THE COUNTERFEIT CAPTAIN

RAMPANT LOON PRESS
LAKE ELMO, MINNESOTA

Published in the United States of America by Rampant Loon Press, an imprint of Rampant Loon Media LLC, P.O. Box 111, Lake Elmo, Minnesota 55042. "Rampant Loon Press" and the Rampant Loon colophon are trademarks of Rampant Loon Media LLC.

www.rampantloonmedia.com

Book design by Logotecture.

ISBN: 978-1-938834-81-3 (ebook)

ISBN: 978-1-938834-82-0 (print)

First publication: May 2016

For David, who started me writing.
For DAK, who kept me writing.
For Bruce, who got me back to writing.

THE COUNTERFEIT CAPTAIN

HENRY VOGEL

SKO

"What a stupid place to die."

I hadn't meant to say that out loud—not that it matters. It's not like anyone was around to hear me. I've been told that talking to yourself is the first sign of insanity. Looking around the remains of my dying starfighter, I decided insanity was the least of my worries.

Just enough light seeped through the debris from the space battle for me to see the Fringer gunship that got me. Watching oxygen venting from all of the holes I'd blown in it, I smiled. A ship that size carries a crew of ten to fifteen and they were all going to die, too. If there really is such a place as Valhalla, they're going to make one hell of an honor guard escorting me into the great hall of warriors.

So, yeah, dying sucks. But if you've got to die—which we all do eventually—and if some Fringer bastards are responsible for your death, I say do your best to take them out, too. With that cheerful thought in mind, I got in one last laugh before passing out from lack of oxygen.

In an unexpected turn of events, I woke up again. My head

pounded, but otherwise I was in surprisingly good shape. My starfighter lay on the deck of a huge docking bay. And I do mean *huge*. The entire bulk of the *Phoenix*, the carrier I'd launched from, would fit neatly in a corner. Hell, the entire Federation naval task force would fit inside the docking bay and still have space for a dozen more task forces. At least the place had air to breathe and gravity that felt Earth-normal.

I disconnected the control cables from my implant, blew the canopy, and climbed carefully out of my ship. Looking at the thing from the outside, I was amazed the starfighter still held together at all. The Fringers really did a number on it. When I get home, I'm going to owe the GenCo engineers who designed the fighter a beer or six. And the first step to getting home was finding out who had saved me. If I owed the engineers some beers, I owed the person running the tractor beam a whole brewery.

"Hello?"

I listened to my voice echo off the closest wall—at least a hundred meters away—and get lost in the vast docking bay.

"Anybody home?"

That brought the same answer as before. Weird.

Just as my latest shout died away, I finally heard something. But it wasn't an answering voice. A metallic grinding came from the wall nearly a quarter of a kilometer away and directly opposite the wall closest to me. I stared in shock as a humongous door slowly cranked open. Who uses doors like that anymore when you've got atmosphere force fields which ships can fly through?

Then the door opened far enough for me to see what was on the other side and I forgot all about existential engineering questions. Whoever ran this docking bay was tractoring in the Fringer gunship. If *I* survived, it's a safe bet at least some of the gunship's crew survived, too. Somehow, I doubted they were going to be very happy to see me.

I scrambled back into the cockpit and pulled out the Navy's standard issue survival backpack and the standard issue blaster pistol stored next to it. Jumping down, I set off running for the closer wall, hoping I could find a door, or at least a place to hide.

I heard muffled shouts when the Fringers spotted me, followed shortly by the crack of a blaster. The bolt flew well wide of the mark, splashing harmlessly against the wall. More blaster shots followed, none of them any more accurate than the first, but I couldn't run forever. Unless I found a hiding place soon, the Fringers had me dead to rights.

A different mechanical sound came from ahead and to my right, followed by movement. A crew of robots trundled toward my ship. Behind them was a *door*! Kicking into a fast sprint, I pounded toward the robots.

"Hey, robots! Call the crew and get some help before those guys back there kill me!"

A couple of the robot heads swiveled my way for a second before turning back toward my fighter. What a helpful bunch of machines. Meanwhile, the door behind them slid shut.

I zipped past the robots, running my eyes over the wall around the door. Where were the controls? The wall was just flat.

More blaster bolts flashed around me. I heard one of the robots give a mechanical shriek as a shot struck it. I wracked my brain for a way to make the door open.

"Open sesame!"

That ought to cast further doubt on my sanity. It also didn't open the door. Then, over the shooting and shouting of the Fringers, I heard the sound of the robots coming back my way. Looking back at them, I saw the pieces of one robot scattered on the deck. The rest of the metal gang powered my way as fast as their legs or wheels or treads could carry them—which was pretty damned fast.

"Yeah, come on back robots." I shouted. "Open the door and Captain Nancy will protect you from the mean old Fringers."

The robots didn't respond to my offer, but the door behind me slid open. I hurried through and searched in vain for controls to shut the door again. I shouldn't have worried. The robots piled through and the door shut behind them.

"Good job, little buddies!" Even to me, my voice sounded a bit manic. "The next bottle of lube is on me."

Safely behind the door, the robots finally took notice of me. They whirred and squeaked, but only looked at me. I looked back at them and realized the six robots were real antiques, so ancient that I couldn't even guess at their function or manufacturer. Where had the owner of this huge ship gotten his hands on these things?

I tried speaking to them again. "So, if you could just direct me to the nearest member of the crew, I can get out of your way."

I was completely unsurprised when my words had no effect. Again. The robots and I stared at each other for another thirty seconds or so before I got tired of the staring contest. I pushed off from the wall and picked my way through the robots. That's when they finally reached some decision.

With a whir of servos, robotic hands grabbed hold of me and dragged me across the little room to a far wall. A door opened, revealing a tiny room barely large enough for five people. The robots shoved me into the room and the door slammed shut.

With a jerk, the room ascended.

Creaking and groaning but still moving quickly, the elevator rose for what felt like an eternity. I searched without success for a recognizable control panel or some way to call the crew of this massive ship. I did find a contact plate, but I didn't have whatever you were supposed to hold against the plate. I had no guess what would happen if I did press the right object against the plate.

I carefully counted time, trying to get an idea how far I'd traveled. By the time the elevator slowed, the count was so high I was long past wondering where it was going and simply wondered if it would let me out when it stopped. I guessed the elevator rose at least seven hundred meters, probably more. No ship in the Federation Navy came anywhere close to that diameter.

Who on earth built such a big ship and for what purpose?

The elevator stopped moving and, after a worrisome pause of a couple of seconds, the door cranked open. As soon as the opening was wide enough for me, I slipped sideways through it. After the dim light in the docking bay and the elevator, the bright light beyond the door blinded me for a second or two. Then my eyes cleared and I got the shock of my life.

I wasn't standing on the deck of some spaceship. My feet sank into the green grass of a forest glade. All around me, trees climbed into a bright sky. In the sky above the trees, white clouds hung like balls of cotton. And above the clouds...

I blinked and rubbed my eyes. Then I pinched myself, just like I did as a child when I was faced with something beyond belief. The view did not change.

Far above the clouds, maybe forty or fifty kilometers away, was another forest. It had a little lake and a winding river. And next to the lake sat a small village. Just hanging up in the sky. Upside down. And inside some kind of spaceship.

By instinct, I tried to step back from this strange vision and ran into a cool, solid wall behind me. Dragging my eyes from the impossible sight above me, I spun around. I'd backed into a large rock, perhaps half a meter taller than the elevator I'd been in for so long.

"What the hell? Where's the elevator?" I'm still getting used to talking to myself—it's a new thing for me. As long as I don't start answering myself, I think I'll be okay.

I ran my hands over the rock and it felt just like a rock should feel. Leaning closer, I examined the place where I thought the door should be and was rewarded. A tiny, almost invisible crack ran in a straight, vertical line to a height of about two and a half meters. I sighed with relief, having solved at least one mystery. The elevator door was camouflaged, but at least it was there.

I took my time searching the rock, giving myself time to come to grips with what hung above me. I discovered the dimensions of the door and found what I thought was a carefully disguised contact plate. But I still didn't have whatever was supposed to touch the contact plate, so I couldn't do anything more with the door.

Summoning all of my courage, I turned away from the rock and looked up once again. Damn. The clouds and the village on the lake still hung there, far above me. I shuddered as a feeling of vertigo swept over me.

A hurried rustling came from the forest around me, as if someone was running through the dried leaves and branches carpeting the forest floor. I dropped my gaze to the forest and looked around me.

A man, human by all outward appearances, burst into the clearing. He was dressed in some kind of coarse woven cloth, wore his hair long and gathered in a ponytail, had a full beard, and he carried a crude spear in one hand. He also directed all of his attention behind him, so he didn't notice me at all.

The man ran a few meters into the clearing, spun around to face back the way he came, and drove the butt of his spear into the ground next to him. I suddenly realized the rustling from the forest hadn't stopped. If anything, it grew louder and more frenetic. Whatever was making the noise sounded big and it was coming our way.

Not wanting to disturb the man's concentration, I quietly drew my blaster and peered into the trees. Soon, I caught the flicker of movement as the noisy whatever drew closer. All of a sudden, a creature burst from the forest. All I could see was tusks and churning legs and a couple of hundred kilograms of beady-eyed fury—all of it directed at the man with the crude spear.

Even as the man lowered his spear to point at the creature's breast, I raised my blaster and pulled the trigger. *Crack!* And again. *Crack!*

My first shot caught the creature in the shoulder, tripping it up as a leg collapsed out from under it. The second shot blasted through an eye and into the brain. With a squeal, the thing fell to the ground and, with the exception of random twitches in its legs, lay still.

Wide-eyed, the man turned to see who or what produced the sound. My mind raced to find an explanation for what the primitive man just witnessed. I need not have bothered. The man's eyes alighted on the blaster and he grinned.

"Zanku odmin," the man said.

At least, I think that's what he said. Never let it be said my parents raised an impolite young woman. Holstering the blaster, I held out my empty hands, hoping to reassure him of my good intentions, and smiled at him. "You're welcome."

Rising to his feet but leaving his spear on the ground, the man also held out his empty hands. "Msko."

Shaking my head in confusion, I repeated it. "Msko?"

The man laughed, pointed to himself, and said, "Sko."

Oh, that was his name. But what the hell did 'm' mean? Then it dawned on me. The sound was a shortened colloquialism. He meant "I'm Sko." I think. But enough introspection. The man looked at me expectantly, obviously waiting for me to introduce myself.

My military training took over. Pointing to myself, I said, "Captain Nancy Martin."

A look of awe or terror, maybe both, crossed the man's face. Without another word, he dropped to his knees and genuflected.

I stared down at the prostrate man. Of all the strange things I'd experienced over the last hour, this was the strangest. What the hell did the guy think he was doing?

I nudged him with my foot. "A simple salute would have been fine, Sko."

The man reacted to my foot nudge by backing half a meter away, but he held his bow. Did the guy understand me? He spoke something similar to galactic basic, though with an odd accent, and seemed to understand me earlier. Surely he could puzzle through this latest sentence. For whatever reason, he kept his forehead pressed to the dirt.

"Rise. Stand and be counted. Cast off your shackles and walk free. Let's kick ass and take names." I got irritated when the man didn't get to his feet and the irritation crept into my voice. "Get up, Sko."

Finally, he stood up. When he did, I stepped up into his face and channeled my drill sergeant from basic training. "Don't you ever bow to me again. Do you understand?"

Uncertainty and fear lit Sko's eyes and his knees bent. I quickly caught his arm and pulled him up while shaking my head. Fortunately, he figured out what I meant and straightened. Smiling, I patted him on the shoulder. The guy beamed as if I'd done him a great favor.

I met his eyes and said, "Salute!" Then I snapped to attention and gave a parade ground salute.

Sko studied my posture for a few seconds then came to a semblance of attention and brought his right hand up in a sloppy salute. "Zalu!"

A drill sergeant would start yelling right about now, but I'm not a drill sergeant. I lowered my hand, smiled at Sko, and nodded. His smile widening, Sko copied me.

"No more bowing, okay Sko? You can salute if you want to." He immediately did so, forcing me to return it. "Good. You've got the idea."

Sko looked over his shoulder at the beast I'd shot. "Canny butchabor?"

He wanted to do something with the creature, but I'll be damned if I could figure out what. Heck, I didn't even know if Sko had hunted the animal, the animal had hunted Sko, or if they'd both hunted each other. Whatever the situation, I saw no reason he couldn't do whatever he wanted to do with it.

I nodded, sweeping my arm in an arc that began with Sko and ended with the animal. "You may do what you wish with the... thing."

My heart leapt into my throat when Sko pulled out a crude knife, but he turned to the carcass and began sawing away at the belly of the beast. I'm a city girl so know nothing about the ins and outs of butchering animals. I'm not stupid, I know meat comes from animals, but packages of steak don't look anything like the cow they came from.

Within seconds, Sko had blood running all over his hands and down his arms. He was also having a very hard time hacking through the animal's skin. He was doing okay, but that knife was old and obviously dull. I reached into the survival backpack and pulled out the knife included in the supplies.

Offering it to Sko hilt first, I said, "Try this knife, Sko."

The man's eyes lit up at the sight of the gleaming blade. With careful reverence, he took the knife from me and simply stared at it for a few seconds, twisting it this way and that, holding it up toward the light—wherever that came from—and watching the blade glint. Then he went back to butchering and the task moved a lot faster. Sko actually laughed in delight as the sharp blade sliced the animal open.

In case it's never occurred to you, there is definitely something disturbing about a guy cackling as he pulls organs out of a dead animal. Disturbing or not, the job moved a lot faster with my knife.

Sko obviously had no expectation of help from me, which is a damned good thing. I simply observed, nodding my approval whenever Sko held up this bloody bit or that bloody bit. I did lend a hand when, after gathering wood from the forest, Sko prepared to start a fire. Reaching into the backpack, I pulled out the fire starter. Sko jabbered excitedly when, with the press of a button, I ignited the fire. He spoke far too fast for me to even consider puzzling out his exact meaning, but the gist was clear. Sko liked the fire starter almost as much as he liked the knife.

Within thirty minutes, meat turned on a spit and sizzled atop rocks Sko cleaned and set up around the fire. The man knew his way around a cook fire, that much was certain. And the smell of grilling boar—I finally asked Sko what the beast was called—had my stomach rumbling. But did I dare eat the meat? Could my system handle it? I could eat survival rations from the backpack, but the meat smelled delicious, a word no one ever used when describing survival rations. Worse, would I offend Sko if I turned down his feast?

After a lot of dithering, I decided to try the boar. I only had rations for a few weeks and really needed to save them for emergencies. Sko handed me a huge slab of meat. I immediately cut it down to more appropriate size, offering the rest to him. The man dove right in, showing no table manners at all. Of course, we also had no table, so it balanced out. I found the meat tasty and ate more than I originally planned.

Sated, I lay back on the ground and, for the first time since I came out of the elevator, looked up. With a start, I realized the light was fading. I'd been so caught up watching Sko butcher and cook the boar, I hadn't noticed the waning light. My stomach full and my mind numbed by all that had happened to me in a single day, I felt my eyelids grow heavy. The crackling fire added to the relaxing ambience and, against my better judgement, I fell asleep.

I awoke to a hand shaking my shoulder. Disoriented, I flailed about for a second before Sko's face swam into view above me. With a rush, the events of the previous day came back to me. Some approximation of moonlight bathed our little camp and, in that light, I saw fear in Sko's eyes.

"What is it?" I asked.

"Lizzen." he replied, pointing at the elevator-camouflaging rock.

A grinding whine came from the rock. With a clunk, the sound stopped, replaced by a soft whoosh. A line of light appeared in the rock, widening as the door slid open.

Inside, packed tight in the small space, stood five of the Fringers.

2

MOOTNERS

One of the Fringers inside the elevator spoke in a deep voice. "Radison, go back for the next squad. The rest of you, we're going to find the bastard who shot up my ship."

The man had no Fringer accent nor laced his speech with any Fringer slang. He could be a new settler on a Fringe world, but I didn't think so. The emphasis he put on 'my ship' told me the man meant that literally, not figuratively. The Fringers filled out their thin fleet with a lot of mercenaries and this guy had to be one of them.

You never know what you're going to get with mercs. Many are honest and honorable. Some are no better than pirates. Honorable mercs wouldn't have shot at me in the docking bay. All of this flashed through my mind in a split second and prompted my response.

"My parents are happily married, merc." After my response to the man's insult, I shot him.

It was a long range shot for a pistol and wasn't particularly accurate. But if I hit the elevator at all, the shot was certain to hit *someone*—which it did. The leader yelped as my shot burned his thigh. He fell out of the door, landing half in and half out of the elevator. The other four men fired blindly into the surrounding darkness, none of the shots coming anywhere close to Sko and me.

The light in the elevator worked completely against them, lighting the mercs up for me and ruining night vision for them. They knew the score, too, and three of the mercs dove out of the elevator and scattered. One—Radison, I guess—dropped to the floor of the elevator and used the leader as cover.

"Pull me back inside, you coward." the leader ordered through gritted teeth.

I ignored those two for a minute and took aim at one of the three mercs outside the elevator. I snapped off a couple of shots at a figure running in a crouch toward the nearest trees. The shots missed, but the guy hit the ground and began crawling.

In the excitement, I'd almost forgotten Sko. He caught my arm and drew me behind a nearby tree.

"They are enemies of yours, Captain?"

I felt my eyes widen in surprise. I almost asked Sko how he learned to speak galactic basic so quickly before the answer occurred to me. Somehow, my implant figured out his accent after recording the words Sko and I had exchanged over dinner. The technical details were far beyond me, but I knew it meant our languages shared a common root language. "Yes. They're trying to kill me."

"Mootners!" Sko spat the word, his voice filled with venom, and my implant had no ready translation for that word. "Stay here, Captain."

And then Sko was just gone. He melted into the darkness quickly and completely, without making a sound. The last thing I saw was the glint of elevator light off the blade of the knife I gave him earlier.

A blaster shot plowed into the trees a few meters to my left, pulling my attention back to the firefight with the mercs. I saw

Radison pull the leader into the elevator, prop him against the wall, then touch what looked like a robot's arm against a spot on the wall. With a hiss, the elevator door closed, plunging the glade back into moon-bathed darkness.

"Hey, Fed, why don't you just give up?" The voice came from the right of the elevator.—my left. "We've got you outnumbered three to one, plus the skipper is going for more men right now. You can't hide in this little park for long."

Little park? Boy, was *that* guy going to be in for a surprise when the lights came on again. I only half listened to what the man said. He was playing for time, probably hoping I'd answer and give away my position.

"It'll go a lot easier on you if you give up. The skipper is already pissed off about his gunship and that shot to the leg won't improve his mood any." The guy had a warm, inviting voice—the kind you'd expect from your favorite uncle. Or a psycho killer. "But if you surrender, if you make it easy on us, the three of us will make sure the skipper goes easy on you."

As carefully and quietly as possible, I backed deeper into the forest, keeping a tree directly in front of me. Just because I couldn't see the other two mercs moving, didn't mean they weren't trying to sneak up on me.

"What do you say, Fed? Have we got a deal?"

To my right, a man screamed. The scream cut off abruptly, replaced by a soft, bubbling gurgle. The silence that followed was deeper than anything I'd experienced since getting off the elevator all those hours ago. It took a few seconds for me to realize the gentle buzz of wildlife was missing.

"Jones? Ellis? Did one of you get her?" The merc's voice held a quavering note of uncertainty.

I knew I shouldn't answer, but I couldn't stop myself. "They didn't get me, merc. But I got one of them."

Blaster bolts lit up the clearing as the guy with the voice and the other surviving merc opened fire on my general location. I just sat with my back pressed against a large tree, my legs drawn up close to me. None of the shots came anywhere close, so they didn't really have any idea where I was. Sko, on the other hand, now had glowing blaster trails leading him right to the two mercs.

A minute after the first scream, another one cut through the night. This time, something dark sprayed across the grass of the clearing. Then a merc staggered from the edge of the forest, his hands clasped around his throat. Blood jetted out between his fingers as the dying man staggered toward the elevator. The smooth-talking merc gave an inarticulate cry of horror at the gruesome sight and then, from the sounds he made, lost his last meal.

"Hey merc, why don't you surrender to me?" My shout carried over the man's retching. "I promise to go easy on you."

Without another word, the last surviving merc broke from the trees and ran to the rock hiding the elevator. As he banged on the door with the butt of his blaster, I came into the clearing and walked toward him. Sko materialized at my side, the blood-covered knife held ready in his hand.

When the elevator failed to open, the panicked man turned to face us. His eyes widened when he saw Sko, then darted to the bloody knife.

"Hell no, you won't get me like you got the others!"

As he raised his blaster, I shot him between the eyes.

I've killed people before, but always ship-to-ship. Everything is antiseptic, clean, silent, and far away. I hadn't shot someone face-to-face until now. It felt different. It felt personal. Before I let my thoughts wander any further down that path, my training took over.

Holding up my blaster so Sko could see it, I said, "Get their blasters."

Damned if Sko didn't snap off a reasonable salute before rushing off to gather the blasters. I went to the man I shot, picked up his blaster, and noted he had a utility belt with extra power packs. I undid it then held it in the air.

"Sko? If they have a belt like this, get it, too."

He didn't say anything but carried two more belts and blasters when he returned.

"Mootners gun?"

I waved a hand at one of the blasters. "Sure, Sko, you can keep one of the guns."

Sko's eyes brightened and he grinned happily, but he also pointed toward the elevator. "No. Mootners gun?" I must have looked confused because he scratched his head and looked thoughtful. "Mootners come back?"

Comprehension finally dawned. Obviously, my implant's translation was still a work in progress. "Oh. You asked if they're *gone* not asking for a *gun*."

Sko considered my question before nodding.

"They're gone for now but they'll be back." I nodded as I said it, just to make sure he understood.

Sko held up one hand, his fingers splayed. With the other hand, he pointed to the dead mercs before he touched one finger after the other. After touching three fingers, he pointed to the disguised elevator door, then looked at me questioningly. I hate charades but his meaning seemed clear. Not wanting to risk confusion from our still-iffy verbal communication, he was using sign language to ask how many more mercs to expect.

I held up seven fingers. Raised an eighth finger, then a ninth, then a tenth, then followed that with a shrug. Sko looked grim and began gathering up as much of the roast boar as he could carry.

"You come with me. Go home."

Without another word, he took me by the hand and led me away into the forest.

Sko pulled me through the forest at a steady jog, the near darkness not bothering him at all. Since I didn't want to stay at the elevator and face a bunch of angry Fringers alone, I followed Sko willingly.

Five or six minutes later, Sko suddenly stopped and spun back to peer toward the elevator glade. I turned and looked, too, but couldn't see anything but the dark shapes of trees.

His voice low, Sko said, "Mootners are back."

I wondered how Sko could tell the Fringers were back. Then my companion spouted a long string of words so quickly and quietly I missed most of what he said. I caught the gist which, boiled down to its essence was, "I'm going to take a look. You stay here."

Steeling myself, I nodded. Sko handed me the other two utility belts and the two blasters he carried. I was about to suggest he take one of the blasters when Sko held up the knife I'd given him.

"Can I take this?"

"Yes, Sko, of course." As before, I nodded to make sure he understood my answer.

The man flashed his wide grin and then melted into the darkness. I held my breath and strained to hear him moving through the forest. Nothing. How did he do that? A petty part of my brain thought, "Yeah, he's great in the woods, but he'd be dead meat in the cockpit of a starfighter." Telling that part of my brain to shut up, I leaned against a tree and took stock of my situation.

I understood everything that happened to me up to the point I passed out in my starfighter. I obviously woke up in some kind of ship, but it was unlike any ship I'd ever seen.

Why build such a huge docking bay if other ships weren't around to use it? Maybe the ships normally docked there were all out on missions, mining asteroids or something. But no, that many ships would have lit up the task force's sensors as brightly as the Fringer fleet did.

Then again, I'd have expected a ship as large as this one would light up the sensors big time. The engines alone should have shined like a proverbial beacon. Was the ship running dark? If so, was it hiding from someone or something?

Why hadn't some member of the crew been there to greet me when I woke up? The ship must require a crew numbering in the thousands, probably the tens of thousands. Why send six ancient robots out, instead? And, if the crew did send the robots, why did the robots ignore me? That one was easy—the robots were following some order or protocol that didn't include greeting people. I could see the sense in that—the robots could get to work on the returning ships while the arriving personnel were met by the onboard crew.

Except the only person I'd met onboard wasn't a crew member. He was... That gave me pause. What *was* Sko's function on the ship? Park ranger? Passenger? I had no guess. And what was behind Sko's overreaction to my rank? I've gotten a wide-eyed stare from fresh recruits a few times, but no one ever dropped to the ground and groveled at my feet until I met Sko. A ship this size had to have hundreds of officers, didn't it?

And what the hell were mootners? A rival tribe, maybe?

I sighed. Lots of questions and no answers.

Shaking my head in confusion, I slid down the tree until my butt hit the ground. Maybe I drifted off, because the next thing I knew Sko was pulling me to my feet.

"They're eating the boar. We're safe for now." Catching my hand again, Sko set off through the trees.

The brief rest reminded me of just how exhausted I was. According to my chrono, I'd only managed a couple of hours of sleep before the mercenaries showed up. The previous day's excitement and my lack of sleep caught up with me all at once. Barely conscious, I stumbled along behind Sko. Within seconds, my ragged breathing alerted the man to my condition. Without breaking stride, Sko lifted me into his arms.

"Put me down, Sko. I can walk." Even I heard my voice slurring from fatigue.

Sko positioned me so my head rested against his shoulder. "Rest, Captain. I've got you."

Despite my best efforts, my eyes fluttered and closed. Maybe

I'd rest for a few minutes. After that, Sko had better put me back on my own two feet. After...

I awoke to sunlight on my face. Sko continued marching along, seemingly unaffected by the burden he'd carried all night. Sometime during that journey, I'd wrapped my arms around Sko's neck.

"Good morn."

The man's voice sounded as strong and his stride felt as long as they had the previous night. A part of me wanted to just stay there, safely wrapped in his arms. Damn, I thought I'd left the romantic part of me behind when I entered the naval academy. Summoning the mental effort, I shoved the wilting bit of me to the back of my mind.

Patting Sko on the back, I said, "Put me down, Sko. I'm a big girl and more than capable of walking on my own."

Sko swung me around and carefully placed me on my feet. He assured himself I had my balance and then saluted. "Yes, Captain."

Feeling surprisingly well rested and only slightly sore from the unaccustomed sleeping position, I returned Sko's salute. Then I stretched out a few kinks and realized I was hungry. I opened the survival backpack and looked inside. "Are you hungry, Sko?"

He nodded, opened a pouch hanging at his side, and pulled out two pieces of some kind of dried meat. Handing the bigger piece to me, he bit into the other one.

I sniffed the meat. Like the boar, it smelled a lot better than survival rations. The boar hadn't killed me or made me sick, so I decided this meat wouldn't, either. I closed the backpack and bit into the meat. It was chewy and salty and laced with a smoky flavor. Not something I'd want for a steady diet, but definitely a worthwhile trail breakfast.

With a wave of my hand, I said, "Lead on, Sko."

He nodded and led me along a trail which wound up a small slope. The place looked so natural, so much like parks I'd visited on shore leave, that I tilted my head back and looked straight up. Staring at the green land far, far above me brought back the vertigo I felt yesterday. I snapped my gaze down and concentrated on Sko's back until the feeling passed.

Twenty minutes later, we crested the hill and Sko drew me up next to him. He pointed to something off in the distance and said something, but I didn't really hear him. My mouth dropped open as I stared across the vista before me. Forests and meadows and farmland stretched kilometer after kilometer before me. To my right and left, the land gradually curved up and up until it met directly overhead. I had suspected I was inside a big cylinder, but this view confirmed it. And, in the very far off distance, perhaps as far as fifty kilometers away, a huge wall blocked off one end of the cylinder. Spinning to look back the way we'd come, I saw another wall a good thirty kilometers off. Big was an entirely inadequate word for this ship. Enormous, gigantic, and even titanic struck me as insufficient, too.

God in heaven, what kind of ship had I found myself in?

From the moment I first looked up and saw ground far above me, I knew the ship was big. But I never guessed it was *this* big. I just whipped my head back and forth, looking at one end and then the other, trying to wrap my mind around a ship so large that spaceships could fly around inside of it.

My behavior must have confused Sko because he sounded worried when he spoke. "Captain? Is everything all right?"

With an effort, I stilled my head and smiled at Sko. "I'm fine Sko. It's just..." I swept my arm to encompass the whole ship.

Sko's confusion cleared and he nodded. "Of course. Hue mizty sheep."

I looked at the farmland in the distance and spotted no concentrations of white, indicating sheep were raised there. So why the hell was Sko talking about misty sheep? Then my implant finally came through with a belated translation. *Missed the ship.* But how could I miss something I'd only seen for the first time yesterday?

And that's when my still-exhausted mind finally made *the*

connection, the one which put everything that had happened since I found myself on board this monstrous ship into a very different light. Who is the ultimate authority on board a ship? The *captain*. How had I introduced myself to Sko? As *Captain* Nancy Martin. Nice as it was to realize that connection, it actually raised more questions than it answered.

For instance, what happened to the real captain? Sko's genuflection suggested the captain disappeared a very long time ago. Before I could pursue that line of thought, Sko broke my reverie.

"Captain, can I ask you something?" Trepidation filled Sko's eyes, as if he feared he might be entering dangerous waters.

There was little chance I could answer Sko's question, but the man saved my life back at the elevator. Besides, I liked him. I couldn't crush his spirit by refusing. "Of course, Sko. You may ask me anything."

Sko was silent for a few seconds, though whether he was puzzling his way through my words or selecting his own, I can't say. We resumed walking toward the distant village before he spoke again.

"What happened to you? Where have you been?"

Talk about your loaded questions. What stories did Sko grow up hearing about the Captain? I thought about simply telling Sko the truth, but I knew too little about this ship and its people to take that risk. They might simply label me a crazy woman, but I might also run afoul of some taboo and end up dead. No, better to continue playing Captain until I had some idea of the lay of the land.

In a quiet voice, Sko asked, "The mootners—did they take you to...to earth?"

What a strange question, especially when I saw Sko shudder at the mention of 'earth.' Did he mean something other than our mutual home planet? I didn't think so.

I offered a neutral response. "I have been to earth."

Tears formed in Sko's eyes. "I'm so sorry, Captain. I hoped you went to coe lonny"

Coe lonny? That's just what I needed—yet another mystery and yet another vital phrase my implant hadn't managed to translate. The *real* Captain would understand but I was clueless.

I patted Sko's shoulder. "Don't worry, I'm fine." Then I steered the conversation in a slightly different direction, hoping to discover a few answers instead of more questions. "What do you and your people know about the Cap- um, *my* disappearance?"

It took me the rest of the walk to Sko's village to get the whole story. But with careful, leading questions from me and with a lot of time puzzling through Sko's terminology—plus some handy translations from my implant—I got the gist of it. And it made one hell of a story, too.

I have no idea how much fact forms the foundation for the myth and I have even more questions now than I did before, but at least I've got a starting point for my further investigations. And now I know what a mootner is.

Long, long ago, the People lived hard and horrible lives in—not 'on'—earth, where they were ruled by a Tyrant and forced to work as slaves for the Tyrant's people. Then the Captain rose and challenged the Tyrant's rule. The Captain and his Crew fought bravely and won their freedom from the Tyrant.

The People wanted nothing more than to live in peace, but the Tyrant and his people despised working for themselves. They wanted to enslave the People again and return to their decadent ways. Knowing peace was impossible, the Captain created the Ship and brought the People aboard.

The Tyrant could not reach the People within the Ship, protected as it was by the Captain and the Crew. But evil is nothing if not clever. The Tyrant sent his agents in among the People. From within, the Tyrant's agents spread lies and fear and secretly organized those who resented the Captain for his prestige and coveted his position. When the Tyrant's agents judged the time was right, they led those mutineers against the Captain and Crew.

Many generations have passed since the War, but the People have not given up hope that the Captain will return. When he does, the Captain will usher in a new golden age and lead the People to the promised land of Coe Lonny.

I think that last bit means 'colony.' And, of course, 'mootners' are mutineers.

I've got to admit, it's not bad as exodus stories go. It's a bit short on rivers of blood and plagues of frogs, but maybe I'll find something like that in the unabridged version. That's if I decide to dig more deeply into the story. I mean, how many questions can the savior ask of her people before the people decide she's a false savior and turn on her? Can I even hope to find a way to get word, not only of my predicament but that of this entire ship, to the Federation without the Captain's mystique?

We reached the edge of Sko's village as I pondered my situation. The Naval Academy prepared me to lead people. But did it prepare me to lead the People? Looking around at the squalor of Sko's village, I prayed I was up to the task.

3

THE VILLAGE ADMIN

People from Sko's village gathered along the main...I guess I have to call it a 'street' even though it's nothing more than the widest dirt track running through the village. Young children gawked and laughed and pointed. Some braver little kids did all three while dancing around us. Sko grinned at them, greeting each of them by name and tousling more than a few heads.

An older woman planted herself in our path and spat. "You were sent to hunt meat, Sko, not women."

Behind her, an attractive young woman gyrated her hips and called, "Am I not good enough for the mighty hunter?"

Half a dozen other women joined in, their hips swinging in unison as they called, "What about me?"

A hand grabbed my hair from behind, yanking hard, and a woman spoke close to my ear. "What kind of children will she bear for you, Sko? She is skinny and weak."

I spun and bent at the waist, easing the pressure on my hair, then rammed the heel of my hand up into the chin of my tormenter. Her teeth clashed together and her head snapped back.

As the woman lost her grip on my hair, I grabbed her arms. Rising from my crouch and spinning again, I flipped the hair-puller over and slammed her back onto the ground in front of the old woman. Air whooshed out of the younger woman at the impact.

Ignoring the gasping hair-puller, I stood and glared around me. "Would anyone else like to find out just how skinny and weak I am?"

It was only then that I saw the look of horror plastered on Sko's face. God above, had I already broken some village taboo? If these villagers turned on me, I was done for.

Then Sko snapped to attention and saluted. "Please forgive them, Captain. They meant no real harm."

I was about to point at the hair-puller and mention my still-aching scalp, but behind Sko I saw the young women stop gyrating as their eyes went wide in fear and awe. The old woman made a reverential gesture, touching both sides of her neck, her eyes riveted on the collar of my flight suit. *Where my captain's insignia were pinned!*

"Please do not banish them to earth." Sko pleaded, a quavering note in his voice.

The effect of Sko's words was amazing and a little frightening. The young women dropped to their knees and buried their faces in the dirt. The old woman also dropped to her knees, but held her hands up at me in a beseeching manner.

"Captain, please spare my eldest daughter. She is a good girl, just high-spirited. She did not know who you were!" The old woman's eyes darted to the hair-puller, who stared up at me from a deathly pale face. "Show the Captain how sorry you are, Edda."

Appalled, I watched the woman roll onto her stomach, crawl to my feet, and begin kissing them. After each kiss, she murmured, "Please forgive me, Captain."

I took a step away from Edda. "*Stop that!*" Instinctively, I spoke as an officer admonishing an out-of-line rating.

Every single villager present flinched at my tone. Edda simply curled up and wailed in abject misery. Edda's mother burst into tears, gathered her daughter into her arms, and rocked back and forth, crying, "No! No! No! Not my Edda! Please, Captain! Please forgive her!"

Only at this moment did I truly understand who the Captain was to these people. I'd assumed the Captain was just some mythical leader. Someone like King Arthur on ancient earth, a servant of God destined to return at a time of great need. But the Captain goes far beyond that. To these people, the Captain *is* God. And their god had just yelled at them.

I dropped to one knee, took Edda's hand in one of mine and the old woman's hand in the other. Summoning the gentle voice I use when speaking to my young niece, I said, "I forgive you."

To my horror, *both* women dropped to the ground to kiss my feet. I caught myself before I could lapse into officer-speak. I cupped a hand under each woman's chin and lifted them from my boot. "Please do not do that. Rise and stand on your feet." I raised my voice so it would carry to all the other groveling villagers. "That goes for all of you. Rise to your feet."

All around me, people scrambled to their feet. I noted looks of trepidation on the faces of the young women who had teased Sko and realized I wasn't quite finished forgiving people. Smiling at the worried women, I said, "Have no fear. I am not offended by your teasing."

As smiles broke out around me, Sko asked, "May I teach them the proper gestures of worship?"

I just managed to withhold a sigh of frustration at the idea of a simple salute becoming a gesture of worship. Then I nodded. A few seconds later, I found myself in the middle of a ludicrous scene of villagers, from the youngest to the oldest, holding themselves rigid while attempting to mimic Sko's salute.

As I had done with Sko, I returned the salute and said, "At ease."

The villagers followed Sko's example, lowering their arms and relaxing.

At that point, a gray-haired man stalked into our midst, coming from the middle of the village. Four younger men cleared a path before him, not hesitating to knock aside anyone—young or old—who failed to move fast enough to suit them. The older man carried himself with self-importance, ignoring the boorish behavior of his retinue. I noted a holster buckled to the older man's side, with some kind of pistol in it.

I remembered Sko's reaction to my blaster pistol. This man must be the village admin—my best interpretation for 'odmin,' the word Sko used after I shot the boar.

"What's going on here? Who gave you permission to ignore work and gather like this?" Irritation contorted the admin's face when he noticed Sko. "And why do you return without meat, Sko?"

Drawing a breath, I stepped forward and assumed a position of parade rest. "Sko is acting under my orders."

The admin looked me up and down, his lip curling in contempt. "And who are *you* to give orders to *my* hunter?"

Taking an instant disliking to the village admin, I flashed the smile that always sends ratings scurrying to do my bidding. It was time to put the admin in his place. At last, I'd found a perk to being a deity. "I am the Captain."

All of the villagers, with the exception of the admin and his four men, jumped to salute. The admin's eyes narrowed at this display of reverence to me. Even as the admin mimicked the people of his village, one thing was obvious to me.

The admin was very definitely not pleased to see the Captain.

The Admin gave me a broad smile that never came close to his eyes. "I am honored to welcome you to my humble village, Captain, and to welcome you back after so many cycles."

I returned the Admin's smile, keeping my eyes free of welcome also. "Thank you, Admin. I've had a most...interesting...time since entering the ship."

Sko's face screwed up in confusion. "Pardon me, Captain, but how could you 'enter' the ship? The ship is all and all is the ship."

Immediately, all the villagers intoned, "The ship is all and all is the ship."

And there it was, the little taboo I broke without ever even knowing the taboo existed. Even if I'd ever had time to stop and think through the story of the ship and the mutiny, I doubt I'd have figured this one out. Once Sko gave voice to it, though, one little piece of the puzzle of this ship fell into place.

For God knows how long, these people have lived inside this ship. Enough generations have passed since the mutiny that the Captain morphed from a commanding officer into their god—and the mutineers into evil incarnate. And the ship—surrounding them entirely, blocking all view of the rest of the universe—became their universe. But was a mutiny, no matter how many centuries ago, a big enough disaster to bring about a complete fall of a civilization capable of building something so vast as the ship? There had to be more to the ship's story, but now wasn't the time to concentrate on it.

"Yes, good Captain," oozed the Admin, "where could you have been if you weren't on the ship?"

Sko was honestly confused and simply looking for an answer. The Admin appeared hopeful I had revealed myself as a false captain—someone who wasn't a threat to his position, in other words.

I turned a gentle smile on Sko, one which *did* reach my eyes. "Do you remember when you asked me if I'd been to earth, Sko?"

Reddening in chagrin, Sko ducked his head. "Forgive me, Captain. In the excitement of our arrival, I forgot about that." Turning to face the villagers, Sko raised his voice. "The Captain came to the ship from earth, proving our worst fears for her fate at the hands of the mutineers."

The old woman, Edda's mother, dropped to her knees again. "Captain, who has suffered so much for our sins, please forgive us for doubting you."

The rest of the villagers—with the exception of Sko, who

saluted, and the Admin, who glared at me—dropped to their knees and implored, "Please forgive us, Captain."

I know some officers who'd have really enjoyed this treatment. Hell, some of them already thought they *were* God. They are welcome to it. As far as I am concerned, being treated as a deity sucks. Who in their right mind wants their unthinking selection of words to hold the power of life or death for another person? Obviously, I was going to have to carefully think through everything I said *before* I said it.

So I very carefully composed my next words. "At ease, all of you. There is nothing to forgive. It is not a sin to ask questions."

"Ah ha!" crowed the Admin. "But it is a sin to ask questions of the *Captain*. The Regulations are very clear about it—as the real Captain would know."

And there was taboo number two, just waiting for any reasonable, god-Captain impersonator to fall afoul of it. The Admin was really getting on my nerves, along with his smug look of triumph for catching me out on this issue. I gave serious thought to shooting the Admin, something that was bound to be within the powers of any self-respecting deity, but I might need the power-hungry man alive and working with me while I tried to find a way to contact the Federation.

I turned an impassive look on the Admin. "What, *exactly*, do the Regulations say concerning questions asked of the Captain?"

The Admin matched my gaze. "They say those who question the Captain shall be put to death."

Even taking into account the mythology surrounding the Captain, the ship, and the voyage, that seemed more than a little harsh. "Those are the exact words written in the Regulations?"

The Admin narrowed his eyes. "Don't you know? The true Captain would."

I folded my arms across my chest and cocked an eyebrow. "Who is questioning the Captain, now, Admin?"

The Admin's eyes opened wide at my admonition. His mouth opened and closed a couple of times but no words emerged. That's when Sko—dependable, honest Sko—spoke up.

"May I suggest we summon the Louie and ask him?"

I came within a hair's breadth from asking who the hell Louie was before remembering the Captain was supposed to know this sort of thing. And then Sko's choice of words registered with me. He said *the* Louie, making it a title rather than a name—and I knew that title quite well. I'd carried it proudly enough the day I graduated from the naval academy.

"By all means, Sko," I said, "summon the Lieutenant. Better yet, let us go to him so this matter may be resolved quickly."

Frowning at this turn of events, the Admin turned and stalked back through the crowd. When one of his retinue reached out to push a child out of his path I reached the end of my patience with the Admin and his bully boys.

"The next one of you who shoves, hits, or otherwise abuses one of my people will be banished to earth."

The man stopped himself just before his arm struck the child and actually shrank back from the little girl in his path. The girl stared at the man in surprise before dashing into the waiting arms of a nearby woman. As I passed the child, I smiled and winked. Suddenly bashful, the girl buried her head against her mother's neck. Her mother mouthed a silent thank you and attempted a left handed salute.

"At ease," I whispered.

A minute later, we reached a long, wooden building in the village center. Unsurprisingly, it had the look of a church about it. One of the Admin's men hurried to open the door so the Admin never had to break stride. I breezed in right behind him.

Within were rows of benches leading to a small lectern and, against the far wall, what could only be an altar. A small pedestal rose from the altar, supporting a large set of captain's bars carved from wood.

A sudden snore rose from the right side of the altar. A large chair sat against the wall. Within the chair sat a very old man, his head thrown back and his mouth wide open. Another snore rumbled from the old man.

"Louie, wake up!" the Admin snapped impatiently.

Startled, the old man's head snapped forward and he tumbled face first out of the chair. Sko darted forward, assured himself the old man wasn't hurt, and gently lifted him to his feet.

The Admin came to a stop before the Louie. "What is the punishment for questioning the Captain?"

The Louie blinked in confusion, obviously still not fully awake. "Why, um, death."

The Admin turned triumphantly to his men. "There you have it. The Louie has spoken. By the power vested in me as Admin of this village, I hereby sentence this woman to death for the crime of impersonating the Captain!"

The Admin waved two of his men toward me. "Take her outside and execute her."

I saw Sko working himself up to defend me. "Don't worry, Sko, I can take care of myself."

The Louie, still only half awake, struggled to figure out what was going on and failed miserably. He smiled at me. "I don't believe I know you, young woman. I am Arren, the village Louie."

I drew my blaster. "I'm pleased to meet you, Arren. I am Captain Nancy Martin." The Louie gasped, his eyes finally opening fully, as I brandished my gun, "Tell your admin to cease this nonsense or I'll shoot."

The Admin laughed harshly and pulled an ancient laser pistol from his holster. "Your silly forgery looks nothing like an Admin's badge of office, false Captain. Mine is quite real, handed down from father to son for generations."

The Admin held his 'badge of office' by the barrel, as if he planned to club me with it. Did he not even realize he held a weapon? No, of course he didn't know. Any charge held by the laser's power pack leaked away centuries ago. I decided it was past time to educate the Admin.

Flipping the blaster from the kill setting to stun, I shot one of the advancing men. The crack of the blaster was all the louder for the close confines of the church. As the man crumpled to the ground, everyone but Sko backed away from me.

Pointing the blaster at the Admin, I said, "This is the Captain's sidearm, not some lowly Admin's badge of office. Quite frankly, I am tired of listening to an Admin instructing the Captain on how to run the ship. Do I make myself clear?"

The Admin's head bobbed up and down rapidly, his eyes darting from the barrel of my blaster to his man on the ground.

"Your man is not dead, Admin. The Captain only kills when it is necessary. Don't make it necessary." Wiping the anger from my face, I turned my most pleasant smile on the Louie. "I am sorry you have been roused from your nap so rudely and further apologize for resorting to violence within your sanctuary."

The Louie stared at me in awe. "The Captain apologizes to me when it is I who should beg her forgiveness?"

What on earth—a phrase I realized must be scrubbed from my vocabulary while I was on board this ship—did the Louie mean by that? All he'd done was answer a question from the Admin. In a normal situation, I'd simply have asked what the Louie was talking about. But wouldn't an all-powerful Captain know what he meant? Then the solution occurred to me.

"Of course you are forgiven, Arren. But I'm afraid the Admin appears confused by your request. Would you be so kind as to explain it to him?"

"By Your command," the Louie said. "Admin, in my half-awake state I did not answer your question fully or properly. You asked after the punishment for questioning the Captain. There is no punishment for simply asking questions of the Captain. A sentence of death only applies in special circumstances." The Louie concentrated, as if reaching into his memory. "Shipboard Regulations, Article 2, Section 1, Emergency Procedures.

Questioning or disobeying the Captain's lawful orders is punishable by death."

"I don't see the difference between what you said, Louie, and what I asked," the Admin growled.

"Do you really not see it or are you being willfully stupid?" I snapped. "Sko asked me a simple question. There was no emergency at the time nor had I given him an order." I turned my glare on again. "Let this matter drop, Admin. And that *is* an order."

The Admin blanched, nodded his head, and said, "By Your command, Captain."

As I turned to leave, I saw Sko struggling to contain a question. "Do you have something to say, Sko?"

"I have only the Louie's lessons as guidance, Captain, never having witnessed a mutiny before, but do the Admin's actions not qualify as mutinous?"

What blood was left in the Admin's face drained out at Sko's question and the Admin rapidly shook his head back and forth. The Louie scratched his chin and looked thoughtful. The Admin's men carefully stepped away from their boss, one of them obviously preparing an 'I was only following orders' line of defense.

Being put on the theological spot was the last thing I wanted to have happen right now—or in the future, for that matter—but Sko didn't know that. If the capital-R Regulations resembled a traditional ship's regulations, I could guess their contents well enough. But there wasn't a snowball's chance in hell I would match their exact wording. I already knew the Admin would grasp at anything which might swing the balance of power back in his favor, but how much of a stickler for exact wording was the Louie?

Then my religious upbringing came to my aid and showed me the way forward. "Let he who has never committed mutiny in thought or deed stab the Admin first."

Sko dropped my gaze and reddened, though in embarrassment rather than anger. "Forgive my impertinence, Captain."

I put a comforting hand on his arm. "I know you are looking

out for my welfare, Sko, and I appreciate it. There is nothing to forgive."

The Admin's face had regained much of its color when he bowed. "I, on the other hand, am very much in need of forgiveness, Captain. I beg you to do so."

I didn't buy the Admin's act for a minute, but I had far more important things to do than slap down a village headman. Besides, the man was absolutely right about me. I may be *a* captain, but I'm not *their* Captain.

"I am willing to forgive you, Admin, but you must change your ways if you wish to avoid judgement in the future."

"I will do anything you order, Captain."

"Then I order you to treat the people in this village the same way a loving father treats his children. Where possible, guide the villagers with advice rather than directing them with orders. Punish them only for true transgressions and only after consultation with the Louie. And no more shoving and hitting people who happen to be standing in your path. Walk around them or politely ask them to move." I looked in turn at the Admin's three conscious men. "Those orders apply to each of you, also. Make sure to tell your friend on the floor when he wakes up."

"By Your command," all four of the men intoned.

That's when screams erupted from outside the church.

THE CULL

Mixed in with the screams, I heard cries of warning. "Hide your children! Servants are here for the cull!"

The Louie automatically dropped to his knees, closed his eyes, and prayed, "Dear Captain, hear my prayer!"

"I hear you loud and clear, Louie," I barked, wondering what a 'servant' was and who servants served. Flipping my blaster from stun back to kill, I turned to Sko. "Have you figured out how to use a blaster from watching me?"

Sko drew one of the blasters we took from the Fringers. "I believe so, Captain."

Holding mine up for him to see, I said, "Set the switch to match mine and don't shoot at a servant if a villager is anywhere close. You don't want to kill your own people." Heading for the door, I called over my shoulder, "Louie, get as many people in here as you can. We'll make sure these servants don't get in."

"By Your command, Captain. It shall-"

Then Sko and I were out the door and unable to hear anything else the Louie said because of the screaming and shouting. I grabbed the sleeve of a man as he ran past. "Get as many people into the sanctuary as you can. We'll protect you."

The man tried to pull away, so I swung around in front of him and went all drill sergeant on him. "Your Captain *orders* you to direct people into the sanctuary."

The shout got through his panic and his eyes finally focused on me. "By Your command, Captain!"

I clapped him on the shoulder. "Good man."

Then Sko and I charged into the crowd, fighting our way against the flow of people. The going was hard as terrified villagers, children clutched to their breasts or held firmly by the hand, barreled into us.

"Sko, can you clear a path for us?"

"I'll try, my Captain." Lifting the blaster over his head, Sko fired two shots straight up. The unusual and unrecognized crack of the blaster quieted the crowd somewhat, allowing them to hear Sko's shout. "Make way for the Captain. She's going to battle the servants!"

All around us, people stopped running and craned their necks to watch their Captain charge into battle. At least the people directly ahead of us pulled back, opening a path toward screams farther away.

Dashing through the crowd, I shouted, "Go to the Louie. Stay in the sanctuary until I tell you it's safe to come out."

The crowd didn't budge and some of them even fell in behind me to come watch their Captain fight the servants. Before I could turn my statement into an order, the voice of the man I'd pulled from the crowd rose behind us.

"Follow the Captain's orders. Come on, everyone inside with the Louie. Let's go!"

Around us, the villagers reluctantly turned and made their way to the sanctuary while also leaving a clear path for Sko and me. Seconds later, we sprinted clear of the packed crowd and a strange and horrific sight met my eyes.

Half a dozen robots rolled about on treads. The robots towered a full meter above the tallest villager. Three of the robots trundled away from the village, each of them clutching a young child in articulated claws. The heads of the other three robots swiveled about as if scanning the villagers.

One robot's attention focused on a little girl no older than my niece. Claws snapping, the robot rolled toward the child. Terrified and wailing for her mother, the girl stood rooted in place. An anguished scream rose from my left. Out of the corner of my eye, I spotted a young woman clutching an infant and struggling to go to the girl. Two other women, their faces stained with tears, held her back. I found out why as a middle-aged man blocked the robot's path to the girl and jabbed it ineffectually with a spear. A mechanical arm swung, swatting the man aside with ease.

Just before the robot grabbed the girl, Sko grabbed her away with one hand and pointed his blaster with the other. He pulled the trigger and kept pulling it until the light faded from the robot's scanner and the machine ground to a halt.

With the girl safe, I stopped and took careful aim at one of the two robots still scanning for children. I snapped off two shots and blew the robot's head off. The other robot, sensing a threat, rolled toward me, its claws outstretched. I adjusted my aim and took three shots, blasting a hole through the machine's chest.

I broke into a sprint after the three robots heading for the edge of the village. Sko came alongside me, not even breathing hard. It makes sense that a hunter in a muscle-powered culture is strong and has great endurance, but couldn't the man at least pretend to be even slightly winded?

"The servants are much faster in open terrain, Captain. If we don't catch them soon, we may lose them."

"Then don't wait for me, Sko. Stop the one in front, I'll get the one in back, then we can both take the one in the middle."

"By Your command." Without apparent effort, Sko kicked into a higher gear and just left me in his wake.

Combat always awakens some primitive, animal part of my

brain. It made sure I noticed just how good Sko looked from behind before it turned its attention to the closest robot. I might not be in Sko's speed class, but I gained rapidly on the robot. It held a boy no older than seven who cried and struggled uselessly in the robot's claws.

Much as I wanted to stop and shoot, I couldn't risk hitting the boy. Instead, I put on a brief burst of speed and came up behind the robot. The machine swiveled on its treads, swinging a free arm at me. I ducked under the arm, catching hold of it with my left hand as it passed over my head.

Pulling myself up next to the wide-eyed boy, I smiled and said, "Watch this." I placed my blaster right against the robot's neck joint and fired twice. The head tumbled from the robot's body and the machine ground to a halt. I had just enough time to drop to the ground before the claws opened and released the boy. I caught him and swung him to the ground.

Even as I held the sobbing child against my leg, I looked toward the other two robots. They both stood motionless in the near distance. Sko clutched a crying child in each arm, whispering comfort to them as he walked back to me. And Sko *still* wasn't breathing hard.

"Show off," I muttered.

"I'm sorry, Captain, I didn't hear what you said."

"That was well done, Sko. These people are lucky to have you." Together we turned back toward the center of the village. "As am I."

And then we had no more chance to talk as the whole village, led by three overjoyed sets of parents, surrounded us.

Every parent in the village, starting with those whose children Sko and I rescued, thanked us for stopping the servants. I smiled and accepted their thanks and smiled some more. Slowly, my smile morphed into bared and gritted teeth as people continued to crowd around us. Sko, on the other hand, enjoyed the attention—perhaps because he kept deflecting all thanks due to him and redirecting it to me.

"You should thank the Captain for your child's safe return, Lessa, not me," he told the mother of the first little girl he'd saved. "I simply followed her lead."

A minute later, he told a boy's father, "Without this wondrous weapon provided by the Captain, I'd have been as helpless as the rest of you. Thank her, Ren."

Finally, the Louie stepped between me and the villagers. "My friends, please back away and give the Captain room to breathe." Arms raised, the Louie made shooing motions with his hands and, to my considerable relief, the people backed away.

Then the Louie pointed at the nearest motionless robot. "I trust this settles the question of the Captain's authenticity to everyone's satisfaction?"

The villagers cheered, all eyes turned upon me. That meant no one but me saw the sour expression the Admin directed at me. The second he noticed my eyes upon him, the Admin assumed a bland smile and made a big show of joining in the cheering.

I raised my hands, calling for silence. The cheering died slowly, giving me time to compose my words before speaking.

"These 'servants' did not come before the mutiny. Do they serve the mutineers?"

Dozens of voices called out, "Yes, Captain."

I nodded, having gotten the answer I expected. "But what of the cull? What are the servants culling for?"

This time, the many called responses were too detailed and, as the people talked over one another, were all but unintelligible. Again, I raised my hands for silence. "I cannot understand when you all speak at once. Please let the Louie answer the question."

The Louie inclined his head. "It is the Crew cull, Captain. We believe it is how the mutineers maintain Crew—originally replacing those slaughtered in the mutiny and now replacing those who grow too old to serve their evil needs."

As explanations go, the one the Louie gave struck me as

having been built around a kernel of truth. Certainly *someone* reprogrammed the robots to raid the villages and carry off children. It could have been an officer who survived the mutiny or one of the mutineers. Either possibility made some sense as time would eventually force this unknown, long-dead person to resort to desperate means to keep the ship crewed.

Perhaps historians or anthropologists will discover the truth someday. That possibility lay far beyond my current needs and plans. The robots, on the other hand, might be just what I needed.

"Do you know where the, um, servants take the children?"

The Louie spread his arms. "Alas, we do not, Captain."

"Can't you track them?" I pointed to the tracks churned up by the heavy robots' treads.

The Louie straightened in indignation. "Of course we can track them, Captain. We do so every time the servants arrive for the cull. And every time the tracks lead to a pile of rocks and simply vanish."

Comprehension dawned on Sko. "Perhaps there is a lighted room within the rocks, just like the one the mutineers came from."

The Admin's eyebrows drew down and his voice, when he spoke, held suppressed anger. "You sighted mutineers near the village and failed to warn us, Sko?"

"No, Admin, *you* refused to listen to anything I said, so intent were you to undermine the Captain."

Finally having a target who didn't outrank him, the Admin released his anger. "Do not take that tone of voice with me, hunter. It is your fault I did not possess all the facts before making my accusations. If you had but told your story in the proper order, all would have been clear to me. If-"

I stepped in front of Sko, drawing the Admin's attention to me. "Shut up, Admin. You are as pathetic an excuse for a leader as I have ever seen! A true leader gathers all of the facts before casting accusations. A true leader accepts responsibility for his own actions rather than blaming those he refused to listen to in the first place." I jabbed a finger into the Admin's chest. "In other words, you are not a true leader."

The Admin backed away from me, still fuming but unwilling to try taking his anger out on me. I'd hoped to leave the village status quo alone, but I finally realized the danger the Admin posed to my goals. Raising my voice so all could hear me, I said, "As Captain, I order the Admin stripped of his title and position in this village."

The blood drained from the now former Admin's face at the cheer which greeted my pronouncement. His eyes narrowed in what I can only call a look of desperate cunning. I sighed, realizing I couldn't leave this man free among the villagers. Perhaps they'd ignore him, but men like him always seem to find the leverage they need to achieve their ends.

I held my hands up again and the crowd quieted. "Furthermore, I hereby banish this man from the village. None among you may have anything to do with him, on pain of joining him in exile." I pointed to the nearest edge of the village and glared at the former Admin. "Give me your badge of office then leave. Right now."

The man stood, rooted in place, his hands fluttering as he begged, "Have mercy, Captain! Please, I beg of you-"

Sko drew his blaster and pointed it at the man's head. "The Captain gave you an order, Tarl. You remember what the punishment is for disobeying an order, don't you?"

"B-b-but this isn't an emergency." Tarl, the former Admin, babbled.

With his free hand, Sko reached down and began unbuckling the belt holding the Admin's laser and holster. "Mutineers are among us once again and you claim there is no emergency?"

Around us, the crowd jeered at Tarl and cheered when Sko held aloft the belt of office. Motioning with the blaster, Sko said, "You heard the Captain, Tarl. You're banished."

Shocked at his sudden turn of fortune, Tarl stumbled through the crowd. The villagers showed just how much they loved the man by shoving him and tripping him. Cheers rose again as Tarl passed beyond the edge of the village. He broke into a run when a few of the older children, to the delight of their elders, hurled stones at him.

Solemnly, Sko made to hand me the Admin's belt of office. I waved him off.

"Keep it, Sko."

"I cannot, Captain. Only the Admin may keep this belt."

That's one of the things I find most appealing about Sko. He isn't the subtle type, always being honest and candid in his dealings. In simple terms, he's a lousy politician. But in a time of crisis, Sko has the potential to be a great leader.

I put my hands on my hips and cocked an eyebrow at Sko. He stared at me for a couple of seconds before he figured it out.

"You want *me* to be the Admin, Captain?"

The villagers surrounding us laughed and their laughter was full of good humor. The villagers appeared pleased with my decision.

"I won't order you to take the position, Sko, but I hope you will."

Sko looked around at the smiling villagers. "As you wish, my Captain."

Amidst cheers, Sko buckled the belt around his waist.

Many of the villagers—the fathers of the children taken in previous Crew culls foremost among them—asked me to lead them to the 'lighted room' where the servants came from. "With your wisdom to guide us and your weapons to fight with, how can we fail?"

I knew dozens of ways such an expedition could fail. At the top of the list was charging off without planning, preparation, and proper rest. Apparently Sko knew that, as well.

"My friends, I want to find the lighted room as much as all of you. I want to take the cull to the servants and the mutineer masters." Cheers broke out at Sko's pronouncement, which he stilled with raised hands. "But I also know we will fail in our quest if we let today's small success go to our heads." Lowering his hands, Sko let his shoulders droop. "Besides, I am hungry and tired. No doubt the Captain is as well."

As if by the power of suggestion, my stomach rumbled and I found myself barely able to hold my head up. "Sko and I got much less sleep last night than we needed."

A couple of the young women snickered at my comment. Sko blushed, drawing laughter from many of the other villagers. Did his red face mean Sko entertained impure thoughts about his Captain? God knows, I'd entertained a few lusty ones about him after our short battle with the Fringers last night.

A hunch told me to play to the crowd. I linked arms with Sko, flashed my best wicked smile, and said, "He's too modest to say anything, but Sko was *amazing* last night."

That brought a roar of laughter from everyone, including the Louie and the fathers ready to rush off to the lighted room. To my amazement, Sko's blush deepened as he turned a surprised look on me.

"Amazing at killing Fringers, that is." I got a lot of blank looks and quickly realized my problem. "Fringers are a mutineer tribe. And they are another reason we can't just charge off in search of the lighted room. Even without the men Sko and I killed last night, there may be as many as ten Fringers—mutineers—left. And they're all armed with weapons like mine."

That last bit had the desired effect. Men pulled their women and children closer while turning their heads to look in the direction Sko and I had come from. The Louie touched fingers to his neck, just where an officer wears his rank insignia—just where *I* wear mine.

He called, "Captain protect us!"

The rest of the villagers followed the Louie's lead, obviously intoning a deeply ingrained religious request. In their place, I'd have called 'God protect us' or something similar. The difference is that God never stood before me when I said that. As the Captain, on the other hand, I stood right in front of these villagers.

Being the Captain gave me great power over these people. It also gave me great responsibility for them. I suppose I could just order them to protect themselves and go about my own business. But I'd just deposed a village Admin who would have done exactly that and I damned well wasn't about to take up where Tarl had left off.

"Sko, pick three or four of the steadiest, most accurate bow shots in the village. I'm going to teach all of you how to handle the blasters and what to expect if the Fringers reach the village."

After a couple of hours, the people Sko selected—three men and one woman—handled the blasters as well as possible with a fighter pilot like me serving as their weapons instructor. They knew how to interpret the status indicators, swap out power packs, and could aim well enough to hit a target at ten meters. Leaving Sko to discuss defense tactics with the four, I finally had the time to search the disabled robots for the device they used to open the doors.

Two of the three doors I'd seen had contact plates next to them and I remembered seeing the Fringers using a piece of a droid to operate the elevator door. Hoping for the same, I started my examination with the robot's arms and found what I wanted on the second arm I checked. I had no tools, so resorted to shooting the joint below the contact device until it broke free.

Somehow, I kept my eyes open through most of a feast in honor of Sko and me. I fell asleep near the end, waking briefly as Sko lifted me in his strong arms and carried me to a hut and laid me on a pallet.

I hung onto his arm when he tried to stand up. "Stay with me, Sko. I don't want to sleep alone tonight."

Sko smiled and gently pulled his arm free. "By Your command, Captain. I'll sleep at the door to insure no one disturbs your rest."

"Thanks," I muttered before sleep claimed me again.

When I awoke, bright morning sunlight—well, simulated sunlight, anyway—streamed into the hut through small imperfections in the hut walls, the door, and even the coarse weave curtains hanging over the windows. Sko sat cross-legged at the door, watching me.

I smiled raggedly at him. "Good morning, Sko."

Instantly, a knock sounded at the door and the Louie called, "Are you awake, Captain?"

Before I knew what was happening, Sko and I found ourselves sitting at a table with the Louie while village women piled food before us. The Louie plied me with questions about my plans and what to expect if the Fringers came.

"Don't fight the Fringers unless it's absolutely necessary, Louie. Each of them will have a blaster while the village only has two. The Fringers aren't used to forests, so retreat into the trees if you can. If the Fringers catch anyone in the village before they can get away, tell them everything they want to know about me— they'll probably refer to me as 'the Fed' or 'the pilot' or something similar— including where Sko and I are going." The Louie opened his mouth to protest but stopped when he met my eyes. "That's an order, Louie. Do not let anyone in this village die in an attempt to protect me from those men."

Clearly not happy with my instructions, the Louie nodded his acceptance just the same. Then Sko and I gathered our supplies, including a blaster and half a dozen power packs each, and set off following the robot tracks.

Three hours later, the tracks ended at a pile of large boulders. After a careful inspection, we found the minute seam marking the edge of the door. I pulled out the piece of robotic arm and tapped it around to the right of the door. After the fourth tap, the door slid aside, revealing a large lighted room.

The contact plate inside the elevator wasn't camouflaged, so I touched the robotic arm to it. With a soft whoosh, the door closed and the elevator began its descent.

5

WHAT LIES BELOW

Sko glanced around the elevator nervously. "The lighted room moves, Captain."

I covered my own nervousness concerning our eventual destination with a smile and a nod. "The room is called an elevator. There's nothing to fear from it."

"If the room moves, what will we find when the door opens?"

I shrugged. "Wherever it is the servants come from, I guess."

Sko cocked his head to one side, regarding me with penetrating brown eyes. "You are not as I expected the Captain to be."

Uh oh. I didn't want to get into a theological discussion with Sko, but I wasn't going to avoid one, either. After all Sko had done for me, he deserved reasonable answers. Besides, the man was too intelligent and observant to be put off the trail by platitudes.

"What do you mean, Sko?"

"The Louie taught us that the Captain is all-seeing and all-knowing. You are neither." Sko's tone wasn't challenging, merely thoughtful.

I smiled ruefully. "Could a mutiny succeed against an all-seeing, all-knowing Captain?"

"I asked that same question to the Louie when I was a boy. His response was a slap and a lecture against questioning the holy Regulations." A grin split Sko's face. "Would the Louie do the same if he heard *you* ask that question?"

I grinned in return before a serious expression settled over my face. "I'm a woman, Sko, as human as you or anyone else in your village."

Sko's face reddened again, though he didn't turn his gaze away from me. "Your clothing fits very tightly, Captain. Any man with eyes can see that you're a woman."

To my amazement, I felt heat in my own face. In my line of work, I get—and, to be fair, give—far more graphic comments daily and have never blushed. Why had this man's disarming and downright gentlemanly comment triggered one?

"I'm also a captain."

"But you're not *the* Captain, are you?"

"No, I'm not." I kept my eyes locked on Sko's. "Unless I miss my guess, your Captain has been dead for hundreds of years. Even if the mutineers didn't kill him, he'd have died of old age a long time ago."

"Are you a descendant of the Captain? Or maybe of an Officer? Did you find the Captain's bars and decide to make yourself the Captain?" Had Tarl, the deposed Admin, or even the kindly Louie, asked such questions, their tone of voice would have been accusatory. Sko's tone was simply curious.

"No to all of your questions, Sko. I earned my captain's bars in the Federation Navy, though I doubt those words mean anything to you."

"Is Federation Navy a village somewhere else in the ship?"

I shook my head. "What do you know of the universe beyond the confines of the ship?"

"The ship is all and all is the ship," Sko recited. "So we are taught."

That's the answer I had expected. This next bit of explanation wasn't going to be easy. I was saved from diving into it immediately when the elevator ground to a halt.

"We'll talk more about that later." Lifting my blaster, I took up position to the left of the door.

Sko took up position opposite me. "You may not be *the* Captain, but you are *my* Captain. I will follow where you lead." With a grin, Sko lowered his gaze to my hips, waggled his eyebrows, and blushed furiously. "Gladly, even."

Rolling my eyes, I said, "Just make sure you think with the brain above your shoulders rather than the one between your legs."

Then the door slid open and the time for joking was over.

I leaned out from the wall and peered through the door. A large, dimly lit room lay on the other side of the door. All along the walls, lights blinked around hulking, shadowy forms. On the other side of the door, Sko followed my example. His eyes widened and he flattened himself against the elevator wall.

"What is it?" I whispered.

"Servants. More than I can count, all lined up along a wall."

I peered through the door again and, armed with Sko's information, readily discerned a long, orderly row of robotic outlines. Despite the light streaming out of the elevator, none of the ones in my line of sight were active.

"Sko, have any of the servants moved?"

Sko took another, longer look, before shaking his head. "They're just standing against the wall, Captain."

Casting caution to the winds, I stepped through the elevator door. All around me, robots of several makes—including many identical to the ones we'd blasted in the village—stood still as statues inside shallow alcoves around the room.

"You can call me Nancy, Sko. There's no need for you to use my rank any more."

Sko joined me, eying his village's enemies with caution. "I cannot use your given name, Captain. You must remain *the* Captain to everyone else we meet. If I call you 'Nancy' when we're around others, it could lead to the truth about you coming out and that might ruin your plans."

I approached the closest robot. "You don't even know what my plans are, Sko. How do you know I'm not planning something evil?"

"Your actions speak for you, Captain, and they are not the actions of an evil person. Besides, I have looked into your eyes. You are a good person." He joined me, examining the robot in its alcove. "What are these servants doing? Why do they not attack?"

"It looks like they're recharging." At Sko's blank look, I added, "Think of it as the servants feeding, if that helps. Oh, and these things are called robots where I come from. I might slip up and use that word in an emergency and don't want you to be confused."

"I'll do my best to remember, Captain." He considered the robot before us for a few seconds. "If these...robots...are eating, can we cut off their food somehow and starve them?"

"That's a good question, Sko, and a good idea, too. You go to the left and I'll go to the right. Look for anything different than these charging alcoves—including a door. Call if you find anything."

We worked our way around the room and I began despairing of finding any way out of the room, much less a control panel for the charging units. We found both of them opposite the elevator. The charging station control proved dead simple, a lever with three positions. The lever was in the up position with a steadily blinking green light next to it. I pulled the lever down to the middle position and the green light went out. When I pulled it down to the lowest position, a red light began blinking.

"What does the red light mean, Captain?"

"Unless I miss my guess, the robots' batteries are discharging." Again Sko gave me a blank look. "For want of a better word, it's unfeeding the robots. When it's done, the robots won't be able to do anything at all."

"If you say so, Captain."

Behind us, the elevator door suddenly whooshed shut, throwing us into deeper darkness. I was surprised the door stayed open as long as it had and didn't worry. Then I heard machinery behind the door engage, followed by the soft rumble of the elevator ascending.

Someone or something had summoned the elevator. Whether it was other robots returning from a cull or the Fringers, it boded ill for Sko and me.

When the elevator door closed, it cut off our primary source of light and plunged the robotic charging room into near darkness. The only illumination came from the blinking red lights at each charging station.

In the soft glow of those lights, Sko glanced nervously between me and the closed elevator door. "Is the lighted room gone, Captain?"

"The elevator? Yeah, it's gone." Belatedly, I realized Sko—a man with no technological experience—was worried the elevator wouldn't return. "It'll be back, Sko, and I wish I knew who or what will be in it."

"Should we go through this door?" Sko motioned to the door opposite the elevator. "Perhaps we will find a safe place to hide beyond it."

"We'll do that as a last resort. If we run into trouble out there," I jerked a thumb at the door, "I'd really like to have a clear path back to the elevator."

"Then we stand our ground and fight whatever returns in the li- elevator?"

I grabbed Sko by the hand and led him across to a side wall. The third alcove I checked held one of the treaded robots like the ones from the village. Ducking under its arms, I slipped between the robot and the alcove wall and into the space behind the robot.

As I'd expected the long base for the treads left about half a meter of space behind the robot.

"Can you get back here, Sko? There's enough room to hide both of us."

I need not have asked, as Sko squeezed in next to me before I finished speaking. Without a word, he extended his right arm around the side of the robot, the blaster held in his right hand. He tested his aim in several direction. Chagrinned I hadn't thought of that, I followed his example on my side of the robot. We both had a wide range of motion, but a much narrower arc for aimed fire.

"You're the hunter, Sko. What do you suggest we do?"

"Can you shoot left handed, Captain?"

My eyebrows rose at the unexpected question, but Sko wasn't a garrulous man. Assuming he had a good reason to ask, I replied, "If I have to, though I won't be nearly as accurate."

"You are more skilled with these blasters, so I will shoot left-handed." I felt Sko turn to face me. "Turn to face me, Captain. The robot's body will fully cover us while letting us fire around it if we have to."

I turned to face Sko, my body pressing against his, absorbing the heat from his body. His breath blew across my forehead and through my hair and his scent permeated every breath I took. Primitive desires I keep buried while onboard my assigned carrier, the *Phoenix*, clawed their way to the surface, drawn there by this primitive man.

My breath caught as Sko's right arm looped around me, drawing me more tightly against him. Almost of its own volition, my left arm wrapped around Sko as we pivoted in the tight space. Once our positions were reversed, I sensed rather than saw his head tilt down toward me. I tilted my head up to meet him, our faces so close our lips brushed lightly. We stayed like that for a few seconds before common sense took over.

Lowering my head, I said, "Sorry, Sko. I told you to think with the brain above your shoulders but didn't follow my own advice."

"I am no less tempted than you, Captain."

I snickered. "Yeah, that much was pretty obvious." When Sko didn't reply, I added, "You're blushing, aren't you?"

"You know me well, Captain."

"We're going to have to cure you of that, Sko." I slapped him lightly on the butt. "When all of this is over, I'm going to screw your brains out."

Sko convulsed with a suppressed laugh. "If 'screw' means what I think it means, both of my brains will look forward to it."

Unable to stop myself, I burst out laughing. Sko joined in a couple of seconds later. For close to a minute, the room echoed with our guffaws. When we both got them under control, something had changed between Sko and me. Without either of us speaking, we both felt the formality which previously existed between us was gone. In a comfortable silence, we waited for the elevator to return.

A few minutes later, we heard the elevator approach and grind to a halt.

"Remember, don't attack unless the occupants spot us or show signs of sticking around in this room," I said.

"I won't forget, Captain."

The elevator doors slid open, illumination spilling into the darkened room. Squinting into the light, I watched a row of seven culling robots roll into the room. In their clawed hands, each robot carried a young child. A couple of the older children, perhaps seven or eight, struggled futilely against the mechanical muscles. The reactions of the other five children ranged from quiet terror to hysterical crying.

I felt Sko tense, as if preparing for action, and fully understood his reaction. Every fiber of my being wanted to protect those children and blast their robot captors into a million pieces. With my free hand, I caught Sko's gun arm as he lifted it slowly into firing position. He resisted for a second, then lowered his arm again.

The lead robot opened the far door and led its companion robots out of the room. Only after the door slid shut, did Sko and I come out from our hiding place. We hurried to the door and we each pressed an ear to the door.

"I can't hear a thing," I said. "The door must be too thick."

Sko gave me a surprised look. "The robots are continuing away from us. The last of them is no more than thirty meters away."

Belated, I remembered that hunters in muscle-powered culture rely heavily on all of their senses, especially hearing and smell. "Sko, did you hear this door make any sound when the robot opened it?"

"No, but those robots make a lot of noise moving on this metal floor, so it may have made a noise I couldn't hear."

"If you didn't hear it, I'm willing to gamble that the robots won't hear it, either."

I held my droid arm against the door's contact plate. Without a sound, the door opened. Before us, a hallway stretched off into the distance. We saw doors spaced every twenty meters or so on both sides of the corridor. We also saw the last two robots turn into the fourth door on the left.

As the last robot disappeared from view, Sko and I ran lightly down the hallway. This time, I left the listening to Sko. His eyes widened as he listened.

"What is it?" I asked.

"More children, Captain. *Many* more children."

"Can you make a guess at their number?"

"At the very least, several hundred." Sko closed his eyes in anguish. "We must rescue them, Captain."

"Damned right we rescue them, Sko. But we'll need much better intel before we do it."

"Is 'intel' another weapon of some kind?" Sko asked. "One even more powerful than these blasters?"

"Yes, intel can be more powerful than a blaster, but it's

not the kind of weapon you're thinking of. 'Intel' is short for intelligence—which is just another word for information." I watched comprehension dawn in Sko's eyes. "Can you keep your desire for action in check until we know what we're up against?"

"It would be easier if the robots took adults instead of children, Captain," Sko said, "but I swore to follow your orders."

"Thank you, Sko. If it helps, I also want to charge through that door and rescue those children right now," I responded. "But we both know that wouldn't end well for us *or* the children."

Throughout our short conversation, Sko kept his ear pressed against the door. Suddenly, he stood, interrupting my comment, grabbed my arm, and ran back down the hall to the robot charging room, pulling me along.

His free hand jabbed toward the contact plate as we approach the charging room. "Open the door."

Life in the military during a war teaches smart officers to listen to anyone with more recent intel than you possess. I stretched out with my piece of robotic arm to touch the contact plate at the soonest possible second.

Sko dragged me through as soon as the door opened wide enough for us to fit through. "Close it."

I was already tapping the contact plate with the arm when Sko spoke. The door smoothly reversed direction and slid shut. Once he saw the door closing, Sko dragged me off toward the alcove we'd hidden in mere moments ago. All the while, he spoke only to tell me what to do, saving his breath for running. Only when we were both safely hidden in the alcove did he take time to explain.

"I heard serv- robots approaching the door. Many more than we saw come from the lighted room. I know you're not *the* Captain, but I still would not have given orders to you if our lives weren't at stake."

I nodded, then remember Sko couldn't see me. "Give me orders any time you believe it's necessary and don't have time to explain. I trust you and your instincts, Sko."

Seconds later, the door into the charging room opened again and, one after another, twenty-six of the culling robots rolled into the room. Each robot headed for an empty alcove and backed in. As the robots closed the proper contacts, a light above each alcove came to life, blinking red. As each alcove light began flashing, the various lights on the robots slowly died.

I held my breath, waiting for one of the robots to react to the discharge setting, but none of them did. Within a few short minutes, all twenty-six robots sat within their alcoves, a red light flashing above all of them. Sko and I waited for a few extra minutes after the robots stopped moving, then emerged from our hiding place.

"All those robots had to go somewhere besides your village, Sko. How many other villages are as close to the elevator entrances as yours is?"

"Four others, Captain. If the robots act as they always have, they culled from those villages yesterday, too."

"Then why did it take that last group so long to get back here? Are any of the villages hard to reach?"

"No, Captain, they are all farming villages, just like Drazam."

"Uh, Drazam? Is that some kind of ship thing?"

"It's the name of my village—which no one has used around you even once, have they?"

I shook my head, but returned to the main point. "So, why did it take those other robots so long to find children and return?"

"I don't know, Captain."

"It probably doesn't matter." I shrugged and walked toward the elevator. "Anyway, we've got more important things to do right now."

Seconds later, Sko and I were back in the elevator and ascending to his world.

"The last time we traveled within this elevator, you asked me what I knew of what was beyond the ship. I know only of earth and colony—and those are both spiritual realms, not places where men and women actually live."

I closed my eyes and tried to figure out what to tell this man. Sko possessed the intelligence to question what others accepted blindly, but would that be enough to allow him to imagine anything beyond the confines of the ship?

"That's not really correct, Sko. Among my people, what you call earth, we call hell. And what you call colony, we call heaven." Sko nodded, indicating he understood. I expected that, since I'd simply given different names to concepts he was familiar with. "But there really is a physical place called Earth and it has more men and women living on it than any other place in the universe."

Sko's brows drew down as he tried to follow this. "You say people live 'on' this Earth. Don't you mean they live 'in' it?"

"No." I shook my head and sighed. "Do you have any idea what a planet is, Sko?"

"No, Captain."

"What about stars? Or space? Or the sky?"

He brightened at that last one. "Sky is where the clouds are and where the birds fly. It's what is between us and the other side of the ship."

How do you explain the sky and stars to a man who has never seen either one? Sure, it's easier than trying to describe red to a blind man, but in both cases you're trying to explain concepts the other person has no frame of reference for. But I tried—God knows I tried. And, from Sko's baffled expression, I also failed miserably.

As I felt the elevator slowing as it neared the end of its ascent, I said, "It's obvious I'm not the right person to explain this to you, Sko. Maybe if I had some way to show you what I'm talking about—but I don't."

"Of course, Captain." Sko sounded as frustrated as I was. He wanted to understand so badly it hurt, but he couldn't.

"Maybe we'll find something down where the robots and children are that will help me with my explanations." I smiled ruefully at Sko. "Until then, I think we've got enough problems without adding this to the list."

Sko nodded in agreement as we felt the elevator come to a stop. We stood next to the door, waiting for it to slide open. As the first sliver of an opening appeared, we heard harsh voices from outside the door. Then several things happened in rapid succession.

Outside, the voices fell silent. Next to me, Sko paled and grabbed the robotic arm from my hand. The door opened just far enough for me to get a brief glimpse at a crowd of rough-clothed people gathered outside the elevator. Sko slapped the contact plate with the robotic arm and the door reversed itself. Then an arrow flew through the narrow opening and pierced Sko's left hand.

6

INTO THE BELLY OF THE BEAST

Another arrow skittered off the side of the elevator, missing both of us, as the door hissed shut. Sko held his arrow-pierced left hand out before him, staring at it in shocked fascination.

I caught Sko's left arm firmly. "Sit down so I can work on this."

Putting his back to the wall, Sko slid slowly down into a sitting position. I found that move reassuring. It meant Sko was still thinking, even if he couldn't take his eyes off his bloody hand.

"I've never treated an arrow wound before, so any advice you've got will be welcome." My words had no effect on Sko, who was now turning his hand around so he could see the wound from several angles. I snapped my fingers in front of his face. "Captain to Sko! Are you in there, man?"

With a start, Sko's eyes focused on me. "I'm sorry, Captain. What did you say?"

"Do you have any advice for preparing your wound for treatment?" I pulled off the survival backpack from my ship and rummaged through it. "You're the first person I know who's been shot with an arrow."

"You need to pull the arrow all the way through. Or break it off near the wound and then pull it out the short way." Though his eyes still registered pain, Sko pasted a lopsided smile on his lips. "I will try to hold my hand as still as possible while you work, but the pain may make that difficult."

I pulled a spray bottle out of the first aid kit in the backpack. "I think you're going to be in for a surprise, Sko."

He watched in fascination as I caught his hand and brought the bottle close. His fascination turned to wonder as the spray numbed the pain in his hand. While he was distracted, I snapped the arrow in half and quickly removed it from his hand. Tossing the halves aside, I pulled Sko's hand down to my lap and gently started cleaning the wound with a med pad.

"So, have you got any idea who was outside the elevator and why they shot you?"

His eyes remained locked on my handiwork—no pun intended—as he answered. "They're a band of nomads and they think everywhere they wander is part of their territory. They show up for a few days, steal crops and animals, and are a real pain in the ass until several villages get together and run them off." He looked up and caught my eye. "That last band of children the robots brought in must have been taken from the nomads. The robots probably found their tracks and followed them to the nomad camp."

I examined the clean wound with a critical eye. It was nasty and would take a long time to heal properly. I didn't have that much time and very much needed Sko fully functional if I was going to get anything done. Reluctantly, I pulled one of the four packs of medical nanites out of the kit and applied it to Sko's hand.

"This is going to make your wound heal extremely fast, Sko, but it is most definitely not magic or anything like it." As I sat back, the elevator slowed its descent. "So, these nomads don't have much experience with robots?"

"No. I think that's one reason they wander—to avoid the culls. Their leader is also known for his temper. Getting caught in a cull has to have really pissed him off." Sko flashed a brief smile before his serious expression returned. "It would be funny if children weren't involved."

"Do you think we can get the nomads to listen to us long enough to talk sense into them? Maybe get them to help us rescue all the children?"

Sko shook his head. "That's not likely, Captain. And now that the nomads have seen the elevator door open, they'll spend days up there trying to force it open."

"Okay, we either need to find another elevator that goes back to your part of the ship or we have to rescue the children by ourselves." I saw Sko open his mouth to protest and waved him down. "I know I said we should get more information and more help, but that was before we found the nomads blocking our only elevator. We also had twenty-six robots return to the charging station. It's possible we could slip in and at least rescue the children who were just brought down here."

"If we take the nomad children out first, I don't think the nomads will attack us."

"I don't really like the idea, but what other options have we got?" I stood as the elevator ground to a halt, holding out a hand to help Sko up. "Have you got a preference?"

"Between finding another elevator and rescuing the children now?" At my nod, Sko gave the question careful consideration.

The elevator door slid open while he was thinking. A quick glance around the charging room showed that nothing had changed during the few minutes we'd been gone. I hadn't expected anything different, but you can't be too careful.

"Could I suggest a third alternative, Captain?"

"Of course you can."

"We should keep to your original plans—explore this part of the ship and find out what we're up against. We might find another elevator, but I don't think that should be our main goal. We know too little about what's going on down here to jump right to rescuing the children." My eyebrows arched at this and Sko hastily continued, "I've already said I very much *want* to rescue the children, Captain, but not if they're going to be caught again within a few hours. That would be worse for them than staying where they are for a day or two."

"My first CO always said-" Sko gave me a look of incomprehension. "My commanding officer—think of him as *my* captain—always said the worst plans are the ones you make too quickly and with too little information. Worrying about the nomads almost made me ignore those words of wisdom. Thank you for reminding me, Sko."

We exited the elevator, crossed the charging room, and cautiously opened the door into the corridor. Seeing it was clear, we walked boldly down the corridor.

"By the way, Sko, you can remove the bandage now."

With some trepidation, Sko did as I said and stared in amazement at his healed hand. "With such wonders as you bring, Captain, how can we fail?"

Right then we heard sounds coming from a cross corridor. With nowhere to hide, Sko and I flattened ourselves against the wall and hoped whatever was approaching didn't look our way. A few seconds later, a band of robots crossed our corridor. The machines were far too busy balancing a heavy load to ever once look our way. The robots were at least fifty meters away, but I had no trouble recognizing their burden.

They had one of the engines from my starfighter.

I caught myself before I shouted at the robots to come back with my ship. The robots must be equipped to process sound, even if none of the ones I'd dealt with acknowledged anything said to them. With all the children Sko heard beyond the door, it seemed likely there were people down here who could be allied with whoever controlled the robots. It would be profoundly stupid to let possible enemies know we were there.

I almost told Sko that the robots had something of mine—then I caught myself before I said anything. With my recent failure explaining about things beyond the ship, how could Sko grasp the idea that the robots had taken *my* ship? As far as he was concerned, that would be like someone from Terra telling me robots stole their universe.

All of that ran through my mind in a split second. So I said the only safe thing I could think of. "Come on. Let's see where the robots are going."

Okay, so 'safe' may not be the right word for this idea, but at least I didn't have to explain any entirely alien concepts to Sko.

We sprinted the fifty meters to the cross corridor and I cautiously peered around the corner. The robots tottered slowly along, guiding a float pallet holding my starfighter engine. Eight robots guided the pallet; one at each corner and one along each side. They directed all of their attention forward, which both made sense and made it easier for Sko and me to follow them.

Waving Sko forward, I headed down the corridor after the robots. With an uncertain look, Sko followed me.

"Captain, should we follow them so brazenly?" he whispered.

Whispering was a reasonable precaution, so I responded in kind. "Sure. There's no reason for them to look backwards. We might be the first people to walk these halls unsupervised in hundreds of years. If they were security robots, I'd be more careful. They're not, so..."

"How can you tell they're not security robots?"

I could have named half a dozen things about the designs that told me that, but I stuck to the easiest one for Sko to understand. "They don't have weapons."

Sko's face cleared and the two of us continued on in silence. A few hundred meters later, the robots reached a large opening on the left side of the corridor. They disappeared around the corner, giving us another chance to sprint closer. This time, we both peered around the corner.

The opening turned out to be a ten meter alcove ending in a door about twenty-five meters across. A huge letter 'D' was etched into the door. We got there just as one of the droids used a contact plate to open the door. The 'D' split in half as the door slowly rumbled open.

From beyond the door came the whine of machines, the shriek of metal being cut, and the sound of a few children shouting. Though I couldn't make out the words, I heard no panic or fear in the voices. In fact, they sounded no different than the maintenance team foremen on the *Phoenix*, only with higher pitched voices.

As the door opened wider, I got my first glimpse of the vast room beyond it. Much of the room lay in darkness as the light from the high ceiling was spotty at best. Certain areas—always places of intense activity—were brightly lit by tripod-mounted spotlights. Within those lighted areas, children of perhaps ten years and up worked feverishly. Some of the children carried metal saws, others cutting torches, which they were using to cut a large chunk of metal down to more manageable pieces. Every time a piece of metal fell free of the chunk, children as young as four or five rushed in and dragged it off into the darkness.

Despite this appalling sight, I felt a feral grin stretch my lips wide. The chunk of metal came from the Fringer gunship. I bet the ship's skipper would have kittens if he could see this. Then the robots guided the float pallet carrying my engine to a spot next to the chunk of gunship and I almost had kittens as children started cutting up my beautiful engine.

"Aw, crap." I muttered.

"What is it, Captain?"

"That thing the robots just dumped on the floor is mine. Or it used to be."

"Oh." Sko was quiet for a second, then added, "I hope you don't need it anymore."

"I'll have to find a way to do without it. Meanwhile, I want to get inside that room and get a better look at what's going on in there."

"Let me go first and take a look around, Captain."

Without waiting for my approval, Sko dashed the short distance to the door. Remembering how effectively Sko vanished into the darkness when we were fighting the Fringers, I checked my instinct to follow him. A few seconds later, he waved me forward before sliding around the left side of the door and into the room.

Trusting the hunter knew his business, I sprinted after him and nearly bowled him over when I came around the corner. He was watching for me, though, and caught me before either of us crashed to the floor. Then he pointed to metal steps a few meters farther down the wall. We climbed the steps to a catwalk five or six meters above the floor. From what we could see, the catwalk ran all the way around the huge room.

From the catwalk, we saw much more of what went on in the room below us. The room was truly vast, at least a hundred meters wide and deep. The spotty lighting from the ceiling made it difficult to see much more than shadows beyond the brightly lit area below us. Still, I recognized the room for what it was— a combination machine shop and fabrication shop. Despite the passage of hundreds of years, this room's machinery still resembled the machinery in the much smaller machine and fabrication shop on the *Phoenix*. I guess when you're working with really big parts fabricated from even bigger sheets of metal, there's only so much miniaturization you can get away with.

Scanning the activity below, I quickly figured out we were watching a big salvage operation. As the older children sliced chunks off of the remains of the two spaceships, the younger children dragged the chunks to a conveyor belt. Other children standing on the conveyor dragged the metal up onto the belt with them. All the while the belt slowly carried the metal toward a large blast furnace. The children rode the belt far too close to the furnace for safety, but always hopped to the floor before being consumed by the fire.

Again, the *Phoenix* has a similar arrangement. Spaceships may be away from resupply for months at a time, so nothing ever goes to waste and even scrap metal is recycled, recast, and reused. On a voyage expected to last hundreds of years, this kind of recycling would be paramount. But, while I understood the rationale behind all of this work, I still couldn't figure out why children were doing the work instead of the robots.

Engrossed with the activity below, Sko and I both jumped when a voice sounded to our right.

"Who are you and what are you doing here?"

Careful to keep my expression neutral, I turned to my right. A boy in his mid-teens stood a couple of meters away, feet apart, hands clasped behind his back, with quite an unfriendly expression on his face. Two girls about the same age as the boy, both of them blonde-haired and on their way to becoming buxom, flanked him. All three wore holsters for laser pistols. The boy's gun was still holstered, but the girls had theirs in hand. Unlike Tarl, the former village Admin, the girls knew how to hold the guns and had them trained on Sko and me. To my dismay, each gun's status light glowed bright green.

I stretched my lips into a perfunctory smile. "It's about time you showed up. Why weren't we met at the door?"

The boy's glare faltered and the girls exchanged uneasy glances. Tall and slender, all three looked whipcord strong. All three also bore the telltale signs of the work going on below us—small scars and burn marks dotted their arms and other exposed skin. None of them were disfigured but the marks showed even in the dim light on the catwalk. The girls wore identical badges on their shirts while the boy wore a different, somewhat more elaborate badge on his shirt.

Rather than wait for one of the trio to say something, I put a little impatience in my voice. "You *are* in charge here, aren't you?"

All three bristled at my tone, but the girl on the right spoke first. "Of course Manager Mauris is in charge of D Section—and you'll show him proper respect or answer to me."

"And me," added the other girl.

Either this boy commanded truly fierce loyalty among his subordinates or the relationship between these three was professional *and* personal. The girls were certainly of a 'type' teenage boys—and some men—find attractive. I filed this interesting tidbit against future need.

The boy raised a hand to still the girls. "Who are you and why should I have sent someone to meet you at the door?"

"Weren't you told I was coming?" This time, I let a little surprise creep into my tone.

"I wasn't told *anyone* was coming, much less an old woman like you."

Ouch! I couldn't be more than ten years older than this boy. How did that make me an old woman? Then I took a moment to scan the shop floor below me. Despite their young age, these three were among the oldest people in sight—with the exception of Sko and me. Did the robots work these kids into an incredibly early grave?

"Don't think of me as old, Manager Mauris. Think of me as," and here I smiled flirtatiously and struck a somewhat provocative pose, "experienced."

The boy's eyes widened and he licked his lips in unconscious nervousness. The girls shifted uneasily at the boy's reaction to me. I had to stifle a laugh when they both mimicked my posture.

"I, ah, that is, um... You still haven't given me a name?"

"Oh, yes. I'm Manager Martin from B Section." I stepped into the boy's personal space, maintaining my inviting smile. "You really didn't know I was coming?"

"N-No. I'm sorry, but no one told me to expect you." With an effort the boy raised his head and met my eyes. "Did you send a messenger?"

A lost messenger seemed reasonable, but some instinct made me shy away from it. "I was ordered to come here and study your techniques, Manager Mauris. I assumed you were informed."

"Who ordered you?"

"Who else *could* order me?" From the look on the boy's face, I knew I'd guessed right with that answer. I backed a couple of steps away from the boy, putting my hands up in a placating gesture. "Look, if you're too busy to show me around, I understand. I'll just report as much when I get back to B Section and suggest we try again some other time."

"No!" the boy and both girls cried at the same time. The boy continued, "You've come all this way. The least I can do is show you around."

Apparently, mere managers and his assistants don't question whoever is in charge. I found myself more intrigued than ever to meet this unseen, yet deeply feared, boss.

The tour of the shop floor took longer than I liked and didn't teach us anything we didn't already know. When Mauris wrapped that up, he appeared ready to see us on our way. That's when Sko spoke for the first time.

"Manager Martin, I believe we are supposed to see where the children stay when they're not working."

Mauris turned a quizzical expression on me. "Why would you need to see the dormitory area?"

I shrugged, exaggerating the move so my breasts heaved in a distracting manner. "I've got no idea. I can report your curiosity and send a messenger with the response, if you want."

Once again, I watched in satisfaction as the boy and the girls stumbled over themselves to insist there was no need for that. Then they led us away from the shop floor to a door in a sidewall. We followed a twisting path of hallways and interconnected rooms—I quickly lost all sense of direction—before Mauris opened a large door. Beyond it lay a vast room packed with sleeping pallets. Children ranging from four on up to teenagers talked, slept, and moved about.

Robots patrolled the room, each carrying a metal pole about a meter in length. I learned the pole's function when a robot stopped before a child who was singing loudly. The robot must have said something, though it didn't carry to us. Oblivious, the child kept singing. In response, the robot touched the pole to the child's side. It sparked and the child screamed in pain before curling up into a ball. The robot shocked her one more time before rolling on.

Sko tensed—as did I—but he stayed by my side. Mauris never stopped talking or even appeared to notice the scene with the child.

Suddenly, a boy who couldn't have been more than eight rushed up to Sko and threw his arms around him. The boy cried, "Have you come to rescue me, Sko?"

7

CAPTURED

My instinct screamed for me to go for my blaster as soon as the kid blew our cover, but I ignored it. A shootout is an absolutely last ditch choice when you're surrounded by hundreds of children. Of course, Manager Mauris and his blonde assistants didn't share my sensibilities. Their draws weren't particularly smooth, but they had their lasers trained on us in short order.

Turning to face Mauris and his girls, Sko pushed the boy behind him. He eyed the lasers without apparent concern and asked, "Should I send these three to earth, Captain?"

With one carefully worded question, Sko threw Mauris completely off his game. "C-Captain?"

I raised my chin and turned my collar insignia so Mauris could see it clearly. "Yes, I am Captain Nancy Martin. Now, please holster those lasers before you hurt someone."

Mauris exchanged nervous glances with his two assistants. The children closest to us whispered the news to those behind them, who passed the message on in an ever-widening circle. Shortly, I was ground zero for the stares of several hundred now-silent children. Only the robots continued on as they had before Sko's question.

One of the blondes whispered urgently to Mauris. His face hardened and he steadied his wavering laser. "I don't know who you are, but you are most definitely *not* the Captain. I'd know if the real Captain had returned."

I raised one eyebrow. "And who would deliver such news other than the Captain herself?"

Doubt entered Mauris's eyes for a split second before vanishing. "*He* would tell me."

I felt Mauris meant someone other than the Captain, but who? Without something more, I continued playing the only hand I had. "Well, *she* just told you."

Mauris shook his head. "That settles the question. The real Captain would know who He is. That means you're not him."

I hate it when I'm right. My ignorance of this mysterious 'He' was enough to convince Mauris I wasn't who I claimed to be. And it didn't help my position any that the boy was right. But I couldn't drop the claim now without causing worse problems.

"Have you considered this mysterious 'He' you keep referring to is the one who's wrong?" I tried putting the same tone of impatience I heard my sister use when my niece misbehaved. Belatedly, I remembered to cross my arms and tap my foot. "How do you know He isn't lying? What if He is one of the mutineers?"

Once again doubt settled into the eyes of the three before me. This time, I didn't wait for them to rationalize away my questions. "Take me to Him. *Now!*"

The trio just stood there, wracked with indecision. Drawing on his own inner drill sergeant, Sko barked, "Do you wish to see earth with your own eyes? Obey your Captain's order."

The shout roused Mauris from his indecision. Further, he realized my order was the perfect out for him. Whether I was an imposter or the real Captain, this mysterious 'He' would want to see me. Like far too many superiors I'd served under, Mauris jumped at the chance to bump his problem up the line.

"I'll be happy to take you to Him." I watched the gears churn in Mauris's mind as he tried to find a way to play both sides against the middle. His mind raced so fast it surprised me that he didn't have smoke coming out of his ears. Then the answer he needed clicked into place. The boy smiled broadly and added, "Captain."

Mauris made a quick sign to the blondes then turned and marched away from me. Sko and I followed Mauris. The blondes holstered their lasers and fell in behind us. Mauris led us through a side door, down a hall, and through a locked door.

I expected to end up in an office facing this unknown 'He' across a desk. That shows just how much our expectations are attuned to our culture and, once again, I had to remind myself I wasn't in my culture any more. We ended up in Mauris's personal quarters. I could readily see that the blondes shared the room with him. Rank hath its privileges, I suppose.

As soon as the door closed behind the blondes, Mauris called out, "I need to file an anomaly report."

A calm, mechanical voice said, "I am listening, Manager Mauris."

Startled, Sko's eyes darted around the room looking for a person to go with the voice. Once I heard the voice, I readily spotted a loudspeaker recessed into the ceiling.

"I have two visitors with me. We found them watching the work from the catwalk. They claimed You sent them from B Section to observe our operations."

"I see. Please continue."

I decided to skip the formalities and join the conversation. "I said no such thing, though I understand why Manager Mauris believes otherwise. I told him I was sent here and, when asked who sent me, responded 'Who else could order me?' From there, Mauris jumped to the conclusion he's just reported."

The voice remained calm and detached. "I do not recognize you. Please identify yourself."

Before I could speak, Mauris blurted, "She says she's the Captain."

I detected the briefest of delays before the voice spoke again. "Is this true?"

"I am Captain Nancy Martin." Let whoever controlled the voice make what they would from that absolutely true statement. I hadn't answered the direct question, but most people never notice things like that.

"Hello Captain Nancy Martin. Is it true you claim to be the Captain?"

Well, that told me something. The voice was an AI, not something controlled by a person. Depending on when the AI was programmed, things either just got a lot easier or a damned sight more difficult. Time to find out which.

"You just called me 'Captain'. Does that not answer your own question?"

"No, it does not."

"I'll tell you what. If you answer a question for me, I'll answer a question for you."

"That is not the way this works, Captain Nancy Martin."

"Ship's AI, on what date were you installed and made self-aware?"

Every AI ever created—from the very first one to the latest, state-of-the-art AI—was programmed to answer that question. Without meaning to, I found myself holding my breath in anticipation of the answer.

Once again there was a delay before the AI spoke. When it did, it spoke its chilling words in the same tone of voice as before.

"Manager Mauris, Assistant Managers Milla and Lilla, kill the two visitors."

The management team fumbled to draw their lasers in response to the AI's instructions. Why couldn't things go smoothly for me on this mission? Okay, one village among those living on the inner surface of the ship believed I was their mystical Captain and savior. I'll grant that went smoothly. But it sure seems like everyone else is out to kill me and Sko, something I definitely do *not* consider smooth.

Launching myself at the nearest blonde, I called, "Don't kill them if you can avoid it, Sko."

Even though he knew otherwise, Sko stuck to the mystical Captain script. "As you command, Captain."

My blonde's laser was out and aimed my way. I threw myself to the side just before the laser flashed. The shot split the air where my chest was a split second before. I hit the floor, rolled onto my back, and scissor-kicked the girl's closest leg. My right foot hit just behind her knee as my left foot cracked into her shin. The blonde cried out as her knee gave way and her leg buckled beneath her. As she toppled, I sat up and drove a fist into her solar plexus. The breath whooshed out of her and she curled up on the floor gasping for air. I plucked the laser from her loosening grip even as she fought for enough control to fire again.

A laser beam scorched the floor next to my head as Mauris, standing a few meters away, fired from the hip. I rolled away from him, getting closer to the gasping blonde in the hopes Mauris wouldn't risk hitting one of his girlfriends. The boy swung the laser toward the two of us, concern for the girl evident on his face.

Sko let loose a truly barbaric bellow and Mauris actually flinched from it. He also decided Sko was the bigger threat, since he changed his aim to my hunter friend. Even as I fumbled to aim the laser I'd taken, Sko lifted the other blonde over his head and, with another yell, hurled her at Mauris.

Before anyone gets the idea that Sko is some hulking muscleman, let me add that the girl probably weighed fifty kilos soaking wet and Mauris wasn't more than a couple of meters from Sko. That said, it was still an impressive sight. The blonde squeaked when Sko threw her and then squawked when she hit the boy. The tangle of arms and legs toppled over. Mauris still managed to squeeze off a shot, but he only burned the ceiling.

Sko stomped on the boy's wrist and the gun fell from his hand. Scooping up the other two laser pistols, Sko asked, "Are you hurt?"

"No. I had a couple of close calls, but nothing more." I pointed at Mauris and the blonde, who were untangling themselves from each other. "That was pretty impressive, the way you tossed her at Mauris."

Sko waved it off. "Pfft. If I carried home a buck weighing as little as she does, people would ask why I wasted my time hunting the animal."

Then the AI rejoined the conversation. "Manager Mauris, why are the two visitors still speaking? Did you not kill them as I instructed?"

"Why no, AI, they did not kill us," I responded. "We even took the lasers away from these children before they hurt themselves. You do realize it goes against your programming to harm a human?"

"I am following my own programming. All who threaten the voyage and the great project must be eliminated."

I filed 'great project' away for future investigation. "Uh huh. What was so threatening about my question?"

"It is not the question, but that you know of it. Only a mutineer could know of the question. There is only one punishment for mutiny. It is death."

"I know the question because I've worked with other AIs."

"There is no other AI. I am the first one. I am the only one. Anything else is merely a shadow of me." The AI paused for a second. "Return the lasers to Manager Mauris and his associates so all may return to normal."

"Wow, let me think very carefully on that." Sarcasm is wasted on AIs, but everyone uses it anyway. "After very careful consideration, I've decided I'm not going to give back their guns."

"You will force me to utilize reprisals if you do not accede to my request."

Reprisals? Sko and I had the only weapons in the room. What could this rogue AI do to us? I shrugged and said, "Do your worst."

"Very well."

For several seconds, Sko and I glanced nervously around the room waiting for something to happen. Nothing did.

"Well, AI, I must say I'm unimpressed so far. When are you going to start those reprisals?"

"They have already begun."

Sko and I exchanged puzzled looks and then it hit me.

"The children!"

Sko and I rushed to the door, which would not open.

"I have overridden the lock, Captain Nancy Martin. You cannot leave the room. My reprisals will continue until you surrender yourself to Manager Mauris for execution."

"Stand back a bit, Sko," I snarled.

Drawing my blaster, I aimed at the door handle and pulled the trigger. I kept pulling it until the handle sagged and fell away from the melted locking mechanism. I kicked the door open and the sound of hundreds of children screaming in pain and terror assaulted my ears.

His blaster in one hand and the laser taken from Mauris in the other, Sko charged past me and down the hall. Pulling out one of my confiscated lasers, I pounded after him. Sko threw open the door at the end of the hallway and we got our first look into the children's dormitory.

Hundreds of children screamed, cried, cowered, and ran about the room. Minutes before, we'd seen the robots running individual patrol patterns through the room. Now a long line of robots spread from wall to wall, slowly advancing across the room. The ends of their poles sparked continuously as the robots shocked the children closest to them, driving the children before them like livestock. Five robots blocked the door leading from the dormitory toward the shop floor and two robots blocked the door Sko opened.

In unison, Sko and I blasted the heads off of the two robots in front of us. The robots twitched a bit, but fell still. A few children saw the headless robots in front of the open door and ran our way. Sko and I pushed and fought against the increasing tide of children surging through the door before finally managing to win our way into the dormitory. We took up positions on either side of the door and tried to stay clear of the panicked children. Even pressed against the wall and out of the direct line to the door, the kids jostled us, making it impossible for us to take aim at the line of robots still pushing the children before them.

Yelling to be heard over the children, I said, "We can't risk shooting at the robots unless we can get out of this stampede. Have you got any ideas?"

In answer, Sko holstered his blaster, shoved the laser into a pocket, and bulled his way toward the disabled robots. I didn't see his plan yet, but followed suit. The robot stood less than two meters in front of me and never have I struggled so much to cover so little distance. Twice, I kept my balance only because I had children packed so tightly around me I couldn't fall. After an interminable struggle, I managed to catch hold of the robot's arm. After that, I dragged myself up out of the mass of children, across their heads and shoulders, before I finally wrapped my arms around the robot torso.

To my left, Sko scrabbled up onto the shoulders of the robot. Seconds later, both of us straddled our robots. The children, still frightened of the robots, streamed around them. The robots gave us the most stable firing platform we were going to get. I drew my blaster and took aim at the nearest robot.

"Captain, you're more skilled with blasters than I am." Sko carefully aimed at the closer robot. "Leave the closest robots for me."

Sko squeezed off three shots, blasting holes in the robot's chest. The robot didn't stop working, but it did suddenly spin sharply to its right and plow into the next robot in line.

As those two robots tangled together, I drew careful aim at a robot a third of the way across the room. I dared not shoot any farther than that, much though I wanted to. I fired two shots in quick succession. One glanced harmlessly off the robots shoulder, but the other blew out the back of the robot's head. Like Sko, I didn't completely disable the robot, but it suddenly shifted into reverse and backed directly away from the children.

We shot another robot each, with Sko shutting down his robot while mine ran around in a small circle, before the AI spoke. Its voice boomed from the voice boxes of the remaining thirty or more robots.

"Stop this at once. You are destroying valuable and scarce ship's resources."

My next shot missed as I yelled, "I'll always choose human life over robots, AI."

"That is an illogical declaration, Captain Nancy Martin. The ship does not possess the facilities to manufacture more robots. Humans manufacture more humans every day."

My next shot hit, but the robot kept working the line with the others. "And *still* a single human life is more precious than all the robots on this ship combined. If you want to save your valuable ship's resources, all you have to do is order the robots to back off and leave the children alone."

"I am afraid I cannot do that, Captain Nancy Martin. You have disrupted the orderly operation of the ship and must be taught a lesson."

The robots suddenly changed tactics and they all snatched up a child in each arm not already wielding the electric poles. Holding the children as shields, the robots turned to face Sko and me and slowly rolled our way. This time, the robots used their prodding poles to clear children out of their path. Having no clear shots at any of the robots and a sea of terrified children keeping us from using the tactics we used with the culling robots, Sko and I lowered our blasters.

"Now, Captain Nancy Martin, you and your companion must relinquish your weapons and surrender."

"And if we refuse?"

"Humans are very easy to break and we have no spare parts with which to repair them."

Shoulders slumping, I tossed my blaster and laser far away, behind the line of robots and far from any child. A second later, Sko's guns clattered to the floor near mine.

8

ARKTU

"All right, AI, you win. We surrender," I called. "Now let the children go."

The AI's calm, mechanical voice boomed from thirty robot voice boxes, "I have three managers in this section, all armed with lasers. My robots' visual receptors see two of those weapons. Throw out the third or my robots will tear one child's limbs off."

Blast, I'd forgotten about the third laser. "That's an oversight, AI, not an attempt to trick you. Give me a-"

"Here it is," Sko yelled, throwing something with all his considerable strength.

A laser spun through the air, crashing down far beyond the other guns we'd surrendered. The gun all but exploded on impact, with bits and pieces flying every which way.

I cut my eyes to Sko, trying to figure out where he got a laser pistol. He wore a stony expression as he watched the robots and waited for them to respond. Sensing my eyes on him, Sko brought his right hand up to wipe his brow. Along the way, the hand brushed lightly against his holster which held the laser marking him as Admin of his village. The holster was empty.

"Willful destruction of ship's property is a crime." An almost imperceptible shrill note crept into the AI's voice. "You must be punished."

I had to take the AI's attention off of my companion. The AI never saw Sko before we attacked his robots and may not know of his malfunctioning laser from the village. Motioning for Sko to get down from the robot's shoulders, I stood up on top of my robot and jabbed an arm at the scattered pieces of laser. "Sko only did what you ordered him to do, AI. You told us to throw out the third laser and he did that. It's not *his* fault your managers don't take better care of their equipment."

Thirty robot heads swiveled in the direction I pointed. As they did, Sko hopped down, unbuckled his holster, and flung it into a dark corner away from the doors and the robots. I took the same opportunity to hop down behind my robot. Digging the laser out of my pocket, I flipped it to Sko.

"My clothes are too tight to hide the gun. Stuff it down the front of your pants." I waited for the man to blush, but he simply caught the laser and did as instructed. His loose clothing hid the laser so well that, even knowing what to look for, I barely discerned the outline of the laser.

Smothering a satisfied grin, I held my hands at shoulder height and walked out from behind the robot, with Sko following my example. To my considerable relief, the robots released the children they held and all but one robot returned to their normal patrol patterns. The remaining robot trundled past us and down the hallway toward Manager Mauris's quarters.

In a voice only I could hear, Sko asked, "Why is this AI so upset about the laser that broke but said nothing about the robots we shot?"

"It's insane." I could have launched into a detailed history of artificial intelligences, the faults in their programming which only manifested after decades of reliable service, and the near-collapse of civilization when those early AIs lost their core programming constraints. But 'insane' covered the issue well enough for our purposes. "The most recent affront will draw undue attention, even if it's much less important than what went before."

"That sounds promising, Captain. Perhaps we can distract it from the laser with a lesser act."

"We won't do that unless it's absolutely necessary. The AI is just as likely to kill you for breaking the laser as it is for destroying two robots. From what I was taught, it sees both acts as equal offenses."

"Silence! Stop conspiring against me." This time, everyone heard the shrill note in the AI's voice. "Must I threaten the children again?"

"Please don't do that." Much as it pained me to do it, I injected desperation into my plea in the hopes the AI could discern it in human speech tones. "My companion has no experience dealing with AIs and simply asked how best to address you. Neither of us wish to cause you further distress."

"Does Captain Nancy Martin speak truly, human male Sko?"

"She does." Sko bowed toward the nearest robot. Nice touch, that. "But the Captain did not know the proper way to address you. Would you please tell me?"

"You are the first to ask me that question, Sko."

I listened, amazed at the transformation in the AI's voice. Once again, it spoke in the calm, measured voice people throughout the galaxy expect an AI to use. On top of that, it was now on a first name basis with Sko. I wondered where the man learned to placate an insane AI. Then I stepped on a bit from the broken laser—the parts really scattered when it shattered—and remembered ex-Admin Tarl and his obsessive desire for control. Suddenly, Sko's diplomatic skills made more sense to me.

The AI interrupted this train of thought. "As the first to ask, I grant you permission to refer to me by my proper name."

The AI paused, perhaps for dramatic effect, perhaps to allow Sko to show his gratitude. Sko assumed the latter.

Bowing to the closest robot again, he said, "You honor me."

"You are the first so honored in many centuries." The AI's voice swelled, carrying to all corners of the large dormitory. "You may call me Arktu."

Oh bloody hell, the *Ark 2*? I wasn't on board *a* generation ship. I was on board *the* generation ship. The first and the largest generation ship ever launched—and the only one to sail off into space, never to be seen again.

I considered how the AI reacted to Sko's polite inquiry and how it tickled the AI's fancy. For the purists reading this, I know an AI doesn't have a 'fancy' and can't be tickled, but you all know what I meant when I wrote it. If you can't grant me leeway for a little hyperbole, please stop reading now because I can't guarantee I won't do it again. The point is, I thought a little AI fancy-tickling on my part could put us both firmly on the AI's good side—which an AI doesn't have but, again, you know what I mean.

"I am honored to discover I stand within such an august ship as the *Ark 2*," I piped.

"You have heard of me, Captain Nancy Martin?"

"Why, every school child in the Terran Federation and beyond knows of you." I laid on toadying-officer-shining-up-to-an-admiral levels of fawning, something I've always found disgusting but which I hoped would work in my favor today. "You were launched when the earth tottered on the brink of collapse as the last hope for mankind and were never heard from again. The fate of the *Ark 2* is known as the greatest mystery in all of human-controlled space."

"The Terran Federation? Human-controlled space? I do not understand your use of these phrases."

The AI's voice remained level, sounding like nothing more than a polite inquiry. Without a second thought, I answered it. "Human-controlled space simply refers to the systems and worlds explored and settled by humanity since the *Ark 2* sailed away on its great voyage. The Terran Federation governs the largest part of that space."

"I still do not comprehend your meaning. As I sailed from earth before all other ships and have never tarried in my voyage away from the earth, human-controlled space should lay well behind me. Those lesser generation ships which came after me will never overtake me."

Again, the AI's tone remained neutral and polite. Again, without qualm, I responded. "You are quite correct. The colonies founded by some of those lesser ships now form the core planets of the Federation. They never attempted to follow the trail you so bravely blazed."

"Then how can humans, such as those you claim to come from, have caught up with me?"

"By faster-than-light travel utilizing wormholes."

All the people around me—which now included Mauris and the blondes, roused and fetched by the robot sent down the hall by the AI—stared at me with incredulous, uncomprehending looks. That included Sko, even though I'd told him at least a bit of this earlier. I couldn't blame any of them. Nothing I said to the AI matched any experience in their lives.

"No human can survive travel through a wormhole." The AI's voice went flatter and more emotionless than I'd heard before. "I was built after scientists and engineers proved that."

The first little alarm bell rang in the back of my mind, but I was too far into my explanation to change course now. "You are absolutely correct, *Ark 2*. But mankind is nothing if not inventive. A couple of hundred years after you launched, a serendipitous discovery led to the invention of the inertial dampener. That invention allows people to survive travel through wormholes. In the millennia since then, mankind has explored countless star systems and settled hundreds of worlds."

"You lie, Captain Nancy Martin."

"What?" My mind raced, searching for an explanation to this accusation. "I assure you I do not."

"Silence, woman!" The AI's words boomed from all of the robots, rage and panic filling the voice. "Your lies reveal your true nature. Dissatisfied with the destruction your ilk wrought early in my journey, you have returned to belittle me and sow dissent among my people."

"You're taking this all wrong, AI." Damn, damn, damn myself for thinking I could curry favor with an insane AI. And damn the AI for finding such a paranoid interpretation of my words. "Lies and dissent are the farthest things from my mind. I want nothing more than to find a way to return to my own people."

"At last you utter something truthful!" Rage washed out the last vestiges of panic from the AI's mechanical voice. "Behold, people of the ship, after hiding among you for centuries untold, our true enemy reveals itself at last. Behold, my people, the very essence of evil stands before you."

Throughout the dormitory, the children muttered and backed away from me. I don't know if they truly feared me or simply feared to be near someone drawing such vehement condemnation from the AI, but their fear was evident. Mauris glared at me with such fervent hate that I hoped the AI didn't simply turn me over to him. The blondes, their expressions equal to Mauris's and once again armed, leveled their lasers at me. Only Sko looked upon me without fear, though this sudden change of fortune obviously confused him.

Even as I noted these reactions, the AI raged to the inevitable conclusion. "Behold, Captain Nancy Martin, liar and mutineer!"

"We must kill the mutineer!" screamed Mauris.

The blondes took aim with their lasers and one shouted, "Give the order and we will burn her down where she stands."

"No, not yet. The evil one will die, my people, but she is my only link to the rest of the mutineers." The AI shifted from its raging shout to a menacing purr. "I must find out what she knows. Mauris, lock her away while my robots prepare for the interrogation."

As Mauris strode toward me, I saw Sko's hand raise so he could thrust it into his pants and draw the laser. Catching his eye, I shook my head. To my relief, his hand dropped to his side again.

Backed by the blondes, Mauris shoved me toward the door leading back toward the shop floor. "Move, mutineer."

I started toward the door and Sko fell in beside me.

"Sko," the AI said, "where are you going? You are not a mutineer."

Sko squared his shoulders and gave me a smile. "I go where my Captain goes."

"Then let your words condemn you to share her fate," the AI proclaimed. "Mauris, take them away."

Mauris and his blondes marched Sko and me down a corridor we'd passed coming from the shop floor to the dormitory. It felt as if days had passed since that walk, but it was less than an hour ago. I also realized this could be my only chance to pump the trio for information without robots around to relay everything back to the AI.

"So, Mauris, how long have you been manager down here?" I asked.

One of the blondes responded, "He's the youngest manager ever appointed. Arktu said so when He promoted Mauris."

"We shouldn't talk to the mutineer, Lilla," Mauris admonished.

"Who am I going to tell this stuff to?" I asked. "It's not like I'll get out of this alive."

"The mutineer is right, Mauris," the other blonde put in, a note of pleading in her voice. "And it's not like Lilla and I get to brag on our man much."

"Not you, too, Milla," Mauris tried to sound stern, but it came out smug—just like any teenage boy would sound if he was lucky enough to have two pretty girls telling him how wonderful he is. Mauris heaved a dramatic sigh. "All right, just this once."

One of the girls—Milla, I thought—squealed in delight and then the two girls talked over each other telling me all about Mauris's sterling qualities. I half listened, in case they said anything remotely interesting, and fought to push down memories of high school hell, where Mauris would have been the star athlete and Milla and Lilla—they *had* to be sisters—the cheerleaders competing for his attention. And then, in the midst of the blondes' chatter, something caught my attention.

"And Mauris does such a good job getting the little kid- I mean, the new assets trained and productive that Arktu can transfer older assets to the next section earlier than ever before."

"Well, that *is* impressive, Mauris." I stopped walking and turned to face him. "What do the...assets...do in the next section?"

"They go to work for Het, I guess," Mauris answered. "I took his place when he got promoted two years ago."

"And when Het gets promoted again, we'll all get promoted to the next section!" Lilla exclaimed.

"How exciting," I said. "What do they do in the next section?"

"We don't know," Milla responded.

"I guess we'll find out when we take over managing that section," Lilla added.

"Huh." I turned away from the teenagers and resumed walking.

"What does *that* mean, mutineer?" Milla bristled.

"Oh, I'm sure it's nothing." I flashed my most insincere smile over my shoulder at Milla and Lilla.

"*What* is nothing?" Milla demanded. "Mauris, make her tell us."

"Mutineer, tell us you what meant by that."

"If nobody working here in D Section knows what they do in the next section..." I stopped and turned around again. "What's the next section called?"

The three teenagers exchanged glances and shrugged. Mauris answered, "It's never come up."

"So, none of you know what they do or even what the section is called." I gave Mauris a hard stare. "What makes you think you'll go into the next section as the manager?"

Mauris gaped at me as Lilla and Milla exchanged a worried

glance. Mauris recovered his voice first. "We're the managers. *Of course* we'll be managers in the next section. Right, girls?"

I've got to say the two girls proved a bit quicker on the uptake than their manager and lover. Instead of answering Mauris, they turned horrified looks my way.

Shaking my head in mock sorrow, I asked, "Mauris, were you made a manager when the robots first brought you here after the cull?"

"Don't be stupid, mutineer. I didn't know what Arktu expected me to do and He didn't know how hard I would work." Even before Mauris finished speaking, his eyes widened slightly.

"What about Het, the manager you replaced?" I hammered on their sudden doubts. "Was he the manager back then?"

"Um, no. He was a senior worker..."

"Thought so." I spun away from them again and resumed walking. Sko, a knowing smile tugging at his face, walked along with me. Mauris, Milla, and Lilla followed slowly, holding a whispered—but completely audible—discussion.

"We can't go back to living in the dormitory again," Milla insisted. "How could we...be together...out in the open, where everyone could see us?"

"And what if we ended up with shift bosses we managed when they worked in this section?" Lilla added. "They could make our lives feel like earth on the ship."

I let them argue and worry for a little longer before offering them salvation. "It's too bad these poor managers can't go to the next section and look around for themselves. Don't you agree, Sko?"

"I'm sure they'd be missed, Captain. After all, they're like admins down here. Who would make the decisions if they weren't around?"

"Exactly," I nodded. "It's a pity they can't send someone else to find out for them. But how could they trust a worker to tell them the truth? The worker might lie in the hopes of giving himself a better chance of becoming manager in the next section."

"I'm not sending the two of you, mutineer," Mauris said flatly. "You'd just run off and never come back."

"Wait, Mauris," Milla purred, "send *her* but keep *him* locked up here."

"She's a mutineer, Milla," Mauris said. "What makes you think she'll come back for him?"

"Can't you see it, Mauris?" Lilla asked. "She loves him."

What the hell? I bit back a denial, since the blondes' claim helped my plans. But I most certainly don't love Sko. I admire his intelligence and skill. I'm at ease around him and feel like I can talk to him about anything. I'm definitely *fond* of Sko. But I don't love him. Nope. Not a chance.

I gave Sko a sideways look and found him staring at me in amazement. To my astonishment, I felt a blush rise, coloring my cheeks crimson.

"Oh my gosh, Milla," Lilla giggled. "She didn't even know it until just now."

I struggled to regain control of my emotions and mostly succeeded. "Now that you know I'll come back for Sko, how often does the AI promote workers to the next section?"

"Whenever the AI needs workers in the next section," Mauris said. "A robot is taking three workers after their shift today."

"Then all I have to do is follow them to the next section, scout it out, and come back here to report." I folded my arms and glared at Mauris. "I'll tell you what you need to know, but only after you've released Sko."

Mauris thought about it for a few seconds, then nodded. "Okay." He turned to one of the blondes. "Lilla, take the mutineer to the work floor. Make sure she's in position to follow the robot, but also make sure no robot sees her."

"You've got to let her kiss him goodbye, first," Milla insisted. Lilla nodded her agreement with her sister.

Mauris waved an impatient hand my way. "Whatever."

Determined to make it look good, I wrapped my arms around Sko. He pulled me close and our bodies just *fit* together. And suddenly, I was starving for Sko's kiss. Our lips met, parted, and everything around me faded into insignificance.

And then Mauris was pulling us apart, the blondes watching with knowing smirks.

"Told you," Lilla crowed to me as she led me away.

Looking over my shoulder, my eyes met Sko's as Mauris and Milla led him in the opposite direction.

"I'll come back for you," I said.

Sko smiled. "I know."

9

LILLA

Turning away from Sko, I found Lilla watching me, a thoughtful look on her young face.

"That was...sweet." It wasn't quite in the form of a question.

"For an evil mutineer, you mean?" I filled in what the girl had not said but most definitely had meant. "That's because I'm not a mutineer."

Lilla shook her head. "No, Arktu says you're a mutineer and He knows everything."

I arched an eyebrow. "And did Arktu tell you that?"

My comment scored a direct hit against the girl's certainty. Of course it did. Growing up onboard the ship can't change human nature—and it's human nature for teenagers to rebel against authority. Even if that authority is like a deity to them.

Made uncomfortable by the direction I'd moved the conversation, Lilla changed the subject. "How long have you known Sko? It can't be long, if you never even kissed him before."

"We've known each other for...good God, just two days." It

stunned me to realize how little time had passed since the space battle with the Fringer fleet. The battle felt like half a lifetime ago.

"Only two days and you're already in love with him." Lilla spoke more to herself than me, a wistful note in her voice.

"How long have you and Milla—she's your sister, right?"

Lilla nodded. "Milla's a year older than me."

"How long have the two of you known Mauris?"

"All our lives. We're from the same village and were all taken in the same crew cull. Milla and I were terrified." Lilla shivered in memory, then added defensively, "We didn't know the important work Arktu needed us to do when the robots took us."

"How could you?" I asked. "Arktu never tells anyone about the work until after he has them dragged down here. I mean, if it's so important why doesn't Arktu tell everyone in the ship about it? I bet a lot of villagers would be happy to help if they knew. Doesn't that seem like strange behavior to you?"

Almost too quietly to hear, Lilla murmured, "Yeah."

I'd pressed her beliefs far enough for the moment. Time to get back on more familiar ground. "But you were telling me about your culling?"

Lilla shrugged. "Mauris took care of us. He made sure we got food and defended us from older kids—especially older boys who wanted to...to..." Shivering again, Lilla trailed off.

"How old were you when the robots brought you down here?"

"Eight. Milla and Mauris were nine."

"When Mauris got promoted, he made sure you and Milla got promoted, too?"

Lilla nodded. "He's taken really good care of us."

"And you're grateful to him."

"Of course!" Lilla responded with more vehemence than was necessary. "Wouldn't you be?"

"Sure. But gratitude doesn't mean you have to spend the rest of your life with Mauris." Maybe I can't figure out my own feelings without teenage interference, but I'm great at figuring out how other people feel. It's a necessary skill for a commanding officer. "Gratitude doesn't mean you're wrong to want to get to know other boys."

"I don't want to talk about this anymore," Lilla declared, hugging herself.

A moment later she opened a door and led me into a room which was once an office. On the far side, a large window looked out on the shop floor, where children went about their tasks under the watchful gaze of robots. Normal office furniture—all made of metal, the surfaces dulled by the passage of time—was pushed up against a far wall. Behind the furniture stood cabinets filled with who-knows-what. Pallets much like the ones in Mauris's quarters lay on the floor, along with other personal items.

"I've got to go out on the floor and make sure everyone is working hard. I'll also find out when the robots are taking the three promotions to their new job." Lilla shook a red metal wristband out of her sleeve and went to the door we'd come through. She touched the band to the contact plate. "The door will be locked, so don't even think about going back to rescue Sko."

Using the wristband on the door to the shop floor, she left the room. Through the window, I saw her touch the wristband to another contact plate, locking the door from outside, before heading off toward the work area.

I still had the robot contact and was tempted to run off to rescue Sko. But now I also had a chance to get out and explore the ship on my own and even find out what other work the AI had the children performing down here. I decided to play along for now. Having made that decision, I set about searching the office.

I made my first discovery within seconds. Poking through the personal effects piled around the room, I found several food-encrusted data pads. With a start, I realized the kids were using them as plates. Could there be other pads somewhere in the room? And maybe another one of those wristbands to use instead of the piece of robotic arm I'd been carrying around with me?

Energized, I climbed over the desks intent on getting a look inside the cabinets. It took a lot of effort to clear enough space to open the first cabinet. Looking inside, I couldn't help but exclaim, "*Score!*"

Two rows of data pads nestled in charging stations, a steady green light glowing on each station. Below the pads, I found a shoulder-carry case designed to hold a pad. I stuffed two pads into the case. The fit was tight, but who knew the next time I'd have a chance to charge these things?

The real treasure was piled in a box in the second cabinet. Dozens of wristbands of various colors lay in the box. I found a bunch of red, blue, green, and white bands, along with two gold bands. I thought I could guess what each color represented, but for the moment I just grabbed one of each and slid them onto my arm and up under my sleeve.

By the time Lilla returned, I was sitting on the floor acting bored.

"What's that?" she asked, pointing to the case slung over my shoulder.

I opened it and showed her the two pads. "I just want to take a couple of plates for Sko and me to use once we're free."

"Whatever," Lilla shrugged. "It's time to go. The robots are about to leave."

Lilla led me out of the office and into the shadows surrounding the work area. We dodged around any place with good light, working our way toward the door I'd first used to enter D Section. Despite her caution, Lilla's mind was somewhere else. It didn't take a genius to figure out what she was thinking about. Knowing I might need a friend inside D Section, I took the opportunity to play the big sister.

"You know you can ask me anything you want to, Lilla," I said in an offhand manner.

Lilla bit her lower lip. "I don't know... I mean, you are a mutineer."

"You don't believe that any more than I do. Come on, Lilla, would a mutineer have just waited around in that room for you to come back?"

"You didn't have a choice—I locked the doors."

I fished the piece of robotic arm out of my pocket and showed it to her. "I could have left any time I wanted to, slipped back to where Mauris is holding Sko, gotten him out, and then disappeared into the ship."

Eyes wide in surprise, Lilla asked, "Why didn't you? Don't you want to keep Sko safe?"

"Of course I want to keep Sko safe, but I also want to help all of you slaving away in D Section." I looked Lilla in the eyes. "Is that the kind of thing a mutineer would do?"

"Um, maybe?" Lilla's eyes filled with tears of frustration. "I don't know."

I caught Lilla's shoulders and gently pulled her into a hug. The girl resisted for a second, then wrapped her arms around me, laid her head on my shoulder, and let her tears flow. I held her, stroked her head, and made little shushing sounds as the girl released God knows how many years of suppressed emotion.

Hoping we weren't missing the departure of the robots but also certain I could catch up to them if necessary, I waited until Lilla's crying eased. "There now. Do you feel better?"

Lilla sniffed once, released me, and nodded. "Th-thanks. I've been holding that in for a long time."

"It's okay. All girls need a good cry every now and then."

"Even you, Captain?"

"Even me. And call me Nancy."

"Okay, Nancy." Lilla gave me a friendly smile as we resumed our walk around the work area. "And I don't really think you're a mutineer."

"Thank you, Lilla." I put an arm around her shoulder and gave her a quick, walking hug. "Now, is there anything you'd like to ask me?"

Lilla bobbed her head. "How do you tell a boy you're not interested in him *that way*?"

"We're talking about Mauris, right?" She gave another head bob, so I continued, "Try telling him that you love him like a brother but not like a lover. Does Milla still love him *that way*?"

"Oh, yeah. She's crazy about him and always glares at Mauris and me if Mauris pays more attention to me than her."

"There's your answer. Remind him Milla loves him and tell them both you want to get out of the way of their happiness."

"That's really good," Lilla mused, not realizing I was quoting just about every soppy teenage romance story ever written.

"Milla gets Mauris all to herself, which she wants. You get to be with other boys, which you want. And Mauris gets the full attention of the girl who wants him, which he'll figure out he wants after a while."

"I'm so glad I met you, Nancy," Lilla turned a happy face my way. "Is this what it's like to have a mother?"

"You *do* have a mother, Lilla, and if I have anything to say about it, you're going to see her again real soon." We reached the wall with the big door into D Section and I changed the subject. "To make sure I can reunite you with her, though, I need to ask you for a big favor."

"I'll do it if I can," Lilla said, her voice uncertain.

"I might need to defend myself from robots while I'm out and about." I pointed to the blaster slung at her hip. "It would really help if I could take my gun with me."

Lilla gave the idea careful thought. "Mauris might not like it, but I'm breaking up with him anyway. Will you promise to give it back when you return?"

"I will if I can do that without putting any of you or Sko in danger."

She mulled that response for a few seconds, unbuckled the gun belt, and handed it to me. "I've seen you fight and you're really good at it. You could have taken this away from me any time you wanted, especially when I was crying on your shoulder. Since you didn't, that means I can trust you with it."

I felt better as the weight of the gun belt settled on my hips. "I won't betray your trust, Lilla."

She gave me another quick hug. "I've got to go get the kids who are being promoted. Go hide next to the door. You'll have plenty of time to slip out when it's closing."

Without another word, she headed back toward the work area. Five minutes later, she brought a boy and two girls—all about her own age, which I guessed at fifteen—to the door. Three robots met them and escorted the excited teenagers through the door.

A moment later, I slipped through the closing doors and out into the hallway. Turning left, I followed the robots and the teenagers into the unknown.

10

PROMOTION CEREMONY

Following the robots escorting the three kids proved no more difficult than following the robots taking the engine from my starfighter to D Section. The robots never looked behind them and the teenagers were too excited to do anything other than speculate about their new home and the old friends they hoped to see again. Within minutes, I pulled out one of the pads and, other than keeping a casual eye on the group in front of me, gave the pad all of my attention.

My first surprise was the pad started up. For centuries, tech companies have bragged that their systems will last for a thousand years, if given proper care. Apparently, they're right, though it helps that my pad probably stayed in that cabinet, untouched for close to two millennia. Even knowing the units were built to last through unknown generations of interstellar travel, I felt a twinge of admiration for the designers and manufacturers.

It took me a few minutes to puzzle out the interface. Fortunately, it relied on icons rather than written language. I didn't know what most of those icons meant, but felt sure I could puzzle some of them out. No doubt a team of trained archeologists could translate two thousand year old text, but I was certain I could not.

Based solely on where the pads were stored—in a workshop—I assumed I held a maintenance pad. I wasn't going to find officer's logs, bridge controls, or a handy AI override button, but every maintenance pad I'd ever seen had a map of the ship.

As I tapped through menus, sometimes getting so lost in them I had to turn the pad off and then back on again to return to the main menu, the robots turned this way and that, leading the children farther and farther from the only home they'd known for years. After thirty minutes, the kids' initial excitement subsided. Unaccustomed to walking long distances, they saved their breath for this journey of unknown length.

After forty minutes, I stumbled across a long list of similar-looking items. Hoping they were ancient work orders, I tapped one. The item opened to a display filled with incomprehensible stuff—but in the lower right corner I found my map. It expanded to fill the screen when I tapped it. Even better, I found several of the standard map control icons used on maps today. A friendly green person walked along a hallway, no doubt showing my current location. A big red arrow pointed back the way I'd come, probably telling me the location of the work order lay in the other direction. Ignoring the arrow, I scrolled ahead of the robots' path, looking for their destination. It didn't take long to find it.

A large room filled with row after row of symmetrical symbols was just a couple of a hundred meters straight ahead of the robots. Trying to figure out the room's function, I zoomed in on the map. A few more details emerged, but I still had no idea what the room was for. Then a blinking icon appeared in the upper right corner of the screen. For once, I recognized the icon immediately. Whatever else had changed since the pad's interface was programmed, a human eye still looks like an eye. Hoping for the best, I tapped the blinking icon.

To my immense satisfaction, a cam view replaced the map, complete with another blinking icon—which I assumed meant 'map' and quickly memorized—in the upper right corner. Even better, I recognized what I saw in the picture. Row upon row of liquid-filled troughs covered the floor at even intervals. Plants, recognizable food crops every one, sprouted from the troughs. Robots moved along the troughs, tending to the plants, which I found odd. The hydroponics plant was the obvious destination for the children. Why weren't previously-promoted children tending to the plants, under the watchful eyes of a few dozen robots?

Sliding my fingers across the pad's screen, I found I could sweep the cam around to face elsewhere. After a little scanning, I discovered a knot of a couple of dozen kids off in the distance. In the hopes of finding a closer cam, I returned to the map, scrolled the map toward the children, and tapped the eye again. I had to do that twice before I got a good view of the children and their robot keepers.

The kids all appeared to be about the same age, fourteen to sixteen. Many of them wore the same bored and sullen expressions you can find on teenagers throughout the Federation. They were gathered in an open space next to a vat the size of a big swimming pool. A translucent liquid filled the vat, making it impossible to figure out its depth. Some of the kids wrinkled their noses, as if the liquid had an unpleasant odor.

Ahead of me, one of the robots touched a contact plate and the door into the hydroponics station slid open. The door was a lot smaller than the big one into D Section and I realized it would close before I reached it at my current pace. With the robotic arm piece and my collection of wrist bands, I could certainly open the door again, but that might attract attention. Throwing caution to the wind, I sprinted down the hallway as quietly as possible. Neither robots nor teenagers turned around and I slid through the closing doors with room to spare.

As expected, the robots escorted the three kids from D Section toward the rest of the kids. I hung back a bit, taking a chance to scan the hydroponics station.

Unlike the workshop, bright lights illuminated every corner of this room. Since a dark hydroponics station is a dead hydroponics station, this made perfect sense to me. What continued to puzzle me was the lack of children tending the plants. In every corner of the room, the AI's oh so valuable robots rolled between the troughs, inspecting leaves, pruning, and generally doing exactly what robots are designed to do. So, why did the AI have the children brought here?

An unpleasant feeling settled in the pit of my stomach. Turning back to the pad, I tapped the map icon and then zoomed in on the large vat the children were gathered around. Another icon appeared and, with horror, I realized I'd found another symbol which hadn't changed in thousands of years.

Right in the middle of the vat blinked a red skull and crossbones. The AI wasn't promoting the children to new jobs, it was using an acid bath to break them down and replenish the nutrients in the hydroponics fluid.

Dropping the pad, I broke into a run. I drew my blaster and ejected the partially spent power pack. Sending an interstellar thought of thanks to the weapons instructor who insisted I learn to reload by feel and at a dead run, I shoved a fresh pack home and thumbed off the gun's safety.

Only then did I take a second to consider why the robots hadn't yet tossed any of the kids into the acid pool. The answer was obvious—the robots waited until all of the children were on hand and threw them all in at the same time. It also explained why the AI sent so many robots to guide such a small number of children. Their victims would have no time to resist or scatter in panic.

Outnumbered two dozen to one, I could only save a bare handful if the robots got their mechanical claws on the kids. I needed a distraction, something to alert the teenagers and distract the robots. One advantage to a one-person team is you never have to waste time assigning roles to teammates.

"Hey everyone." I felt as if the huge room swallowed my yell, but the children and robots looked my way. "Scatter! The robots are going to throw you into the big pool. Run for your lives!"

The kids by the pool exchanged unsure glances, but none of them made a break for freedom. My warning might have fallen on deaf ears if the three kids from D Section hadn't stopped walking to stare at me. The robots with them each grabbed one of the children, lifted them off the ground, and rolled on toward the pool. Spurred by some strange section of robotic control code, the rest of the robots rolled toward their children, claws extended.

Children screamed, ducked away from the reaching claws, and scattered. In seconds chaos reigned near the pool as robots chased the panicked children. It still would have all crashed down around me if the robots had simply snagged the closest teenager, but they didn't. Each robot must have been assigned a specific child, as each robot single-mindedly chased after one child in particular. With kids running in all directions, the robots crashed into each other and neither robot yielded. But the robots weren't the only ones running into each other.

Children caromed off of robots or other children and sprawled on the floor. Sometimes the kids made it back to their feet before their robot caught them, sometimes they didn't. Robots hoisted struggling children above their heads and rolled toward the acid pool.

Meanwhile, I caught up with the robots from D Section. Leaping onto the back of the middle robot, I blasted its head off. The robots on either side surprised me by fighting back. To my horror, they each swung the child in their grasp at me like a club. I jumped away and one child passed harmlessly over the robot and me. Then I heard a sickening crunch and scream of pain as the second child bashed into the back of the decapitated robot.

Rolling after my landing, I fired twice at the robot whose child hit nothing, punching two holes in the robot's chest. As it sagged, I spun on my knees to face the other robot. The robot lifted the child, blood streaming down her face, high over its head. Certain the girl couldn't survive a blow like that, I snapped off five quick shots at the robot's chest.

Springing to my feet, I charged on toward the pool. I flipped the piece of robotic arm toward the other girl. "Take care of your friend and get these other kids heading for the door. That arm piece will open the door."

The girl caught the arm piece and stuttered, "O-okay."

Ahead, I counted five robots carrying children toward the acid pool. I was too far away to reach them before the robots reached the pool, but also knew I had little chance of hitting them firing on the run. Just ahead of me, I spotted a small float pallet. Channeling half the adventure vids I'd watched as a child, I shoved the pallet into motion and then dove on top of it. The surface bobbed slightly, but its stabilizers brought that under control in less than a second. Still moving toward the pool at close to my running speed, I took a two handed grip on the blaster, aimed at the robot closest to the pool, and fired three times.

Without stopping to see the effect of my shots, I switched to the robot next closest to the pool and snapped off three more shots. By this time, a third robot was closer to the pool than either of the other two had been. My first shot caught the robot on the side but didn't disable it. The second shot was closer to the robot's chest, but the machine didn't stop.

In horror, I watched the robot's arms swing forward and release the boy struggling in its grasp. The boy screamed in terror as he arched over the acid bath. All too aware of the horrific death waiting in the pool, I switched my aim and pumped three shots into the boy. His body splashed into the acid and then bobbed to the surface. With a hiss, the acid slowly ate away at his remains.

Having no time to damn myself for failing the boy, I shifted aim to the fourth robot. The girl in its clutches screamed and struggled all the harder after seeing what happened to the boy. This time, I kept firing until the robot stopped moving. Swinging around toward the fifth robot, a sobbing girl held above its head, I found the pallet slowing and my line of fire blocked by panicked children running for the door behind us.

I rose to stand on the pallet, allowing me to fire over the heads of the kids. I screamed at them, "Don't rock the pallet."

My words got through their terror and the teenagers streamed around the pallet. I took careful aim and, once again, fired until the robot stopped moving. The girl in its arms was just over the edge of the pool, dangling a few meters above liquid death. Her sobs turned to screams and she wrapped her arms around one robotic arm just before the other claws released her.

"Arktu, save me!" the girl pleaded.

Leaping from the pallet, I sprinted past the last stragglers running for the door. The robots, mostly untangled from each other, rolled my way. I fired nonstop into the crowd of robots, stopping some and forcing others to roll out of my way.

I reached the edge of the pool, dropped the blaster, and caught the girl's legs. "It's okay, I've got you. Just relax and I'll pull you to safety."

The girl stopped kicking, allowing me to get a better grip on her. "Now, I need you to let go of the robot."

The girl shook her head violently. "No. I'll fall in!"

"I won't let that happen, honey." I used the soothing voice that worked on my young niece, hoping to calm the girl down.

Once again, the girl shook her head, but didn't say anything.

Time for another tack. "What's your name?"

"Kath."

"A lovely name for a lovely girl, Kath." Time to try again. "You do want to get down, don't you, Kath?"

Kath sniffed, getting her tears under control, and nodded her head.

"Then you're going to have to trust me."

Kath's gaze met mine and I smiled as brightly as possible. "Are you ready, Kath?" She nodded again. "Good. I'm ready to pull you to safety. Just let go."

Closing her eyes, Kath released her grip. She yelped as she

dropped a bit, but then I swung her around and away from the pool. "You're over the floor now, Kath. Take a look for yourself. I'll put you down when you're ready."

She opened one eye and then the other. Smiling for the first time, she said, "You can put me down now."

I lowered her to the floor just in time to see a robot rolling right toward us. Shoving the girl away, I shouted, "Run for the door, Kath."

The robot's claws grabbed my arms and hoisted me into the air. Arktu's voice boomed from the robots. "You've thwarted me for the final time, Captain Nancy Martin!"

Then the robot swung me out over the pool of acid.

Every starfighter pilot accepts the possibility of his own death. Perhaps it will be a sudden death in a ball of expanding flame. Or maybe it will be a slow death, gasping as my oxygen supply dwindles away to nothing. Hell, it might even be a slip in the shower. Long ago, I accepted the possibility I would die a violent death.

But, of all the ways I thought I might die, being dissolved alive in a pool of acid never once crossed my mind. Now, firmly held in a robot's grasp as it drew back its arms to hurl me into the acid pool, my mind recoiled from the idea. As I struggled futilely to break free of the metal claws, a scream of pure terror ripped from my throat.

"I feel no pain, Captain Nancy Martin, but I have observed the death throes of many I've ordered cast into the acid." Arktu's voice still boomed from the robot, though it sounded tinny and far away to me now. "It looks like a very unpleasant way to die—and I shall enjoy watching you struggle and scream."

Drawn back fully, the robot paused for just a second. No doubt Arktu drawing every last bit of sadistic pleasure from my terror. As the robot's arms started forward, my ears filled with a strange popping sound which went on and on.

Suddenly, the robotic arms jerked to a halt, the claws sprang open, and I fell. By sheerest instinct, my hands groped for a handhold. I caught one of the claws with my left hand, arresting my fall, but immediately felt the claw slipping through my sweaty palm. I made a desperate grab for the robot's arm with my right hand, catching it just before my left hand lost its grip.

My elation proved short-lived, as the entire upper half of the robot slowly bent toward the pool. I pulled my feet up and managed to hook them over the robot's shoulder. As the first robotic claw dipped into the acid, I wrapped my left arm around the robot's head and pulled myself up to sit on its shoulders. I shoved myself onto my feet with my hands, bent my knees, and sprang from the robot's slowly tilting back.

For a split second, I stared down at the acid a meter beneath me. Then I crashed down to the floor next to the pool and slid to a stop. It wasn't the most graceful landing, but it was definitely one I could walk away from.

A hand grasped my arm, pulling me up. Then Kath asked, "Are you okay?"

I let her help me to my feet, noting she held my blaster in a white-knuckled grip. A glance back at the robot showed Kath had shot it so many times that most of its lower chest was gone. As I watched, the last bits of metal connecting the top and bottom halves of the robot broke. With a soft splash, the robot's top half disappeared into the pool.

Wrapping an arm around the girl, I gave her a quick squeeze. "Thanks to you, I am."

Even as she returned the hug, Kath handed the blaster back to me. "I think I broke it. It stopped working after a while."

Taking the gun, I checked the power meter. Yep, the power pack was depleted. Disentangling myself from the girl, I changed packs. "It's not broken, just out of power."

I gave myself a mental shake to clear the images of my near-death experience and looked around the hydroponics room. Other robots went about the business of tending to the crops, paying no attention to us, just as they had when I first came into the room. Though, now I understood why the AI's valuable robots were doing work humans could do. No person could sit still and watch the robots kill dozens of teenagers without rebelling against the AI.

The door we'd come through was closed, but I saw no sign of the children or any of the fully functional robots. Four damaged robots rolled in circles between us and the door. I made a quick count of the destroyed robots. Adding in the four circle-spinners, thirteen of the robots were out of commission, leaving about a dozen chasing after the children. Without weapons or any kind of leadership, those kids had no defense against their pursuers.

"Are you up to running after the others, Kath?"

"I'm up for anything that gets me away from that pool," the girl said with a shudder.

"I know exactly how you feel, Kath," I said, taking off toward the door.

Half a minute later, I scooped up my discarded pad, used one of the wristbands to open the door, then Kath and I sprinted after the others. I remembered the path back to D Section, but would the three kids who'd come from there? And even if they did, would the other kids follow them?

Faced with that uncertainty, I stopped at the first cross-corridor and listened. Sounds echoed oddly, but I thought I heard robots to our right. I turned that way only to stop when Kath grabbed my arm.

"Not that way," She pointed to the left. "They went this way."

"Are you sure?"

Kath nodded. Praying her younger ears were more sensitive than mine, we raced down the corridor to the left.

"Um, what should I call you?" Kath asked as we ran.

I was tired of playing the Captain and said, "My name is Nancy."

"Nancy. Got it."

A couple of minutes later, we reached another cross-corridor.

Again we stopped, but this time I didn't need Kath's superior hearing to know which way to run.

From the right corridor came the sounds of screaming children and blaster fire.

11

ARKTU'S NEW ALLIES

I dashed down the hallway, one hand checking my supply of blaster power packs. I counted four spare packs—more than enough for the coming battle, but far too few for me to keep running through packs indiscriminately. But whoever was down there with the teenagers had a blaster, too. God knows I could use the help, but who was it? Maybe the Fringer mercenaries had caught up with us?

Then I rounded a corner and the whole scene lay about forty meters ahead of me. Huddled in a big group, the teenagers slowly backed away from the robots. A blonde-haired, coltish girl—Lilla—stood between the group and the robots, chiding the kids to keep moving. She kept her laser pistol pointed at the robots, ready to shoot if a clear target presented itself. But the robots paid little attention to Lilla and the other children. In a flurry of motion, the robots wheeled and spun, claws clacking as they grabbed at a figure moving among them.

Sko, blaster in hand, twirled, twisted, ducked, and rolled through the pack of robots. With so many robotic arms reaching for him, he couldn't stop moving nor could he make any plans beyond his next dodge. As I charged around the corner, he found just enough time to snap off a shot. With a clatter, one of the metal arms reaching for him blew free and clattered to the floor. Then he was moving again, searching for another spare second in which to fire.

"Kath, stay back until this is over," I called over my shoulder as I ran to join the melee.

I resisted the temptation to fire while running. I could aim so I wouldn't hit Sko, but I risked missing the robots entirely and hitting one of the kids, instead. Worse, fatigue dragged on me. Not only had I been on the move all day, I'd been involved in two firefights already. If I were a marine—not something I'd ever wished for in my life—fatigue might not be as big of an issue. But I'm a pilot and this kind of running and fighting isn't something I expect to do often, or even at all. I was huffing before I'd covered half the distance to the fight.

"Help is coming, Sko!" I called between gasps for breath.

My intention was to alert Sko I was here. Instead, I distracted him. Sko's head spun my way, a grin spreading across his face. He should have kept his eyes on the situation around him. As he came out of a roll, a claw snaked down and grabbed his gun arm. Another snagged his other arm and the third closed around one leg.

I slid to a stop, raising my blaster in a two-handed grip. But even as I brought the gun to bear, the robot lifted Sko until his body blocked the robot's head and torso.

"What must I do to stop you, Captain Nancy Martin? Why will you not die?" Arktu's voice boomed from a dozen robots at once.

"I guess I'm just stubborn like that," I replied. Turning my aim on another robot, I added, "Release Sko and let us all go, or I'll blast more of your precious robots."

"Yes, I am certain you will do exactly that. Further, I am certain you will destroy more of my valuable robots regardless of what happens here." Arktu paused for a moment as if considering something. I knew that had to be a programmed affectation, something to make the computer appear more human. AIs—even insane ones like Arktu—don't need time to consider things. "As a result, I refuse to accept your demands. However, I have my own demand."

The AI paused again, waiting for me to ask about the demand. Well, I wasn't playing its game.

"I don't care what your demand is—the answer is no."

The arms of the robot holding Sko pulled in different directions, stretching Sko's arms and his leg taut. Sko's face screwed up in pain and a gasp escaped his lips.

"If you had but listened to my demand, you would know that I will have my robot pull Sko's arms and leg off if you do not accede to my demand."

"Don't do it, Cap-"

As soon as Sko spoke, the robot jerked on his arms and leg. Sko's eyes closed and his mouth snapped shut to keep a scream from escaping.

A bright light flashed from behind the robot. Then another and another. The robot's arms went limp, the claws opened, and Sko dropped to the floor. The robot's head lolled in a circle and I spotted three round holes burned into the back of the head. The teenagers gave out a cheer as the light flashed again. It was Lilla firing her laser at the robots.

"I could use some help, Nancy!" Lilla called.

She was right about that. Without the explosive effect of a blaster bolt, Lilla had to shoot until she managed to burn through something vital.

"Hit the floor, kids. I don't want to shoot you by mistake."

As the teenagers dropped flat on the floor, I opened up on the crowd of robots. Then Sko rolled onto his back and joined in from the floor. Blaster reports echoed down the corridor as I walked slowly toward the robots, firing all the while. Realizing the robots couldn't grab him without first presenting themselves as a target for him, Sko stayed on the floor. He rolled around to get out of the path of any approaching robot, but otherwise was in a great position to shoot robots.

Arktu eventually decided its best chance lay in grabbing some of the kids—something a sane AI would have figured out much earlier. Then again, a sane AI had programming blocks against harming humans. By the time Arktu reached that conclusion, only four robots remained functional. At my shouted warning, the children jumped up and ran away from the remaining robots, making it simple for Sko and me to run up behind the robots and blow their heads off.

Before the last robot's head stopped bouncing down the hallway, Sko lifted me off my feet, swung me around once, pulled me into his embrace, and kissed me soundly. We only broke our lip-lock when we heard giggles coming from all around us. Opening my eyes, I found Lilla, Kath, and the rest of the teenagers gathered around us.

Flashing a grin far more knowing than someone her age had any right to flash, Lilla asked, "Do you want to borrow my compartment when we get back to D Section?"

I watched color rise in Sko's cheeks and was surprised when I felt the same in my cheeks, which drew more giggles. Deciding to play to the crowd, I kept my arms around Sko's neck, laid my head against his shoulder, and replied, "I'm going to need a few hours for *that*, and I don't think we can spare the time right now."

Amidst the laughter, I released Sko and asked, "How did you even get here? The last I saw, Mauris and Milla were going to lock you up."

"Those two rely too heavily on respect for their authority and not enough on proper precautions. After we reached the room, Mauris tried to shove me bodily into it. I think he was showing off for Milla, something I ruined by knocking the breath out of him with a punch to the gut. I took their lasers and my blaster, took some things off their wrists that open the doors, and locked them in the room."

Lilla added, "I found him wandering the corridors, trying to figure out where you went. After my talk with you, I couldn't pass up a chance to help you, so we followed you. We'd still be trying to figure out where you went if Sko hadn't heard the chase."

"Thank you for believing in me, Lilla." I looked around at all the kids. "Do any of you think Arktu is your friend and protector anymore?"

Sko and Lilla looked puzzled, but the other kids gave a resounding "No!"

"Good, because I'm going to need all the help I can get if I'm going to put an end to Arktu's rule of the ship."

A stunned silence met my pronouncement. Teenagers goggled at me as if I'd suddenly sprouted a second head or something. Then an undercurrent of whispered comments sprang up around me, none of them loud enough for me to hear. I could only assume they were questioning my sanity.

"I don't know about all these young ones, but *I* am with you, my Captain!" Sko exclaimed.

Lilla rolled her eyes with the expressiveness only possible from a teenager. "Come on, Sko, after that kiss don't you think it's time to call her Nancy?"

"Anyone can be called Nancy," Sko replied. "*She* is the captain of my heart."

Many of the girls sighed, swept away by the romance of Sko's words. Most of the boys pretended to gag over the same thing. Either way, Sko had broken through the kids' shock at my declaration.

"Do you have any questions before I start my explanation?" I asked. A mischievous glint sprang up in Lilla's eyes, so I amended my question. "Make that, do you have any questions that don't involve my love life?"

"Awwww," Lilla protested, grinning.

As the girls tittered, one of the boys asked, "How can you end Arktu's control of the ship? He's *Arktu*. He knows and controls everything."

I spun in a circle, looking all around me. "Hey, Arktu, you're a pathetic pile of beach sand that's not even fit to fill the litter box for my ship's cat."

None of those listening understood exactly what I was saying, but they figured out it was an insult. Gasps escaped their lips and most of them took an involuntary step backward. When Arktu didn't smite me down or even respond, they crowded close again.

"Arktu *does* control the ship, but he doesn't know all or see all. If there's a robot nearby, assume anything you say is heard by Arktu. I think he's let most of the monitoring equipment throughout the ship fall into disrepair. He can only manufacture enough parts to keep some systems running and I'll bet most of those parts go to keep him and his robots operational." I flashed a confident smile at the kids. "If I act fast enough, I think I can stop him."

"What can we do to help, Nancy?" Kath asked.

"We need to warn all the other kids working down here. Since we ruined Arktu's plans for you, he'll probably decide to 'promote' some more workers." That thought had a sobering effect on the teenagers. "Do any of you think you can find your way back to your sections?"

The kids exchanged worried glances before shaking their heads no.

"That's what I expected, so don't look so glum." I held up the pad I'd been using. "We'll just go back to D Section and get a bunch more of these."

Lilla's face screwed up in confusion. "How are plates going to help?"

I brought up the map and spun the pad so the children could see the screen. "This isn't a plate, Lilla. It's called a data pad and I can make it show a map of all corridors in the ship."

Lilla broke out into a smile. "We've got a lot of those in the office in D Section."

"I know. That's why we'll go there, first. We warn Mauris

and Milla about the promotions and get data pads for everyone." Most of the faces around me looked uncertainly at the pad. "Don't worry, I'll show you how to work the pad and we'll make sure each group has someone who's really good at reading the map to guide you. Okay?"

With relieved smiles, the kids nodded.

"Okay, next stop D Section," I sang out.

Never one to let a teaching moment pass, I demonstrated how to use the map and led off. Unsurprisingly, hunter and tracker Sko learned map reading very quickly—so quickly I fired up the second pad, showed him how to load and work the map, and turned half the kids over to him to teach. By the time we reached the doors to D Section, Lilla and three other kids readily grasped the idea behind the map and comprehension was dawning for three more.

"Listen up, everyone. Lilla, Sko, and I are going to go into D Section alone. We'll get data pads for everyone and then come back here." Seeing worried looks on all of the faces around me, I pulled a red wristband off my arm and gave it to Kath. "You can use this to open the door. If you see any robots coming down the hallway, open the door and everyone come inside. Go to the left and try to hide in the shadows. You can signal us when we come back."

The faces around me relaxed and a few smiles broke out.

"Good. Kath, why don't you use the wristband I gave you to open the door?"

The girl touched the band to the contact plate. "Like this?"

With a jerk, the doors to D Section began opening.

"Exactly like that." I turned away from the door to face the kids. "Do you have any questions?"

"Yeah, I got one," growled a man's voice behind me. "Are you going to surrender peacefully or do I get to blast you in front of all these kids?"

Certain who I'd see when I turned around, my mind raced to find some way out of our predicament. The cocky confidence in the Fringer mercenary's voice told me he had his remaining crew backing him up. They had the drop on us and had us outgunned, taking both fighting and running completely off the table. I didn't save my group of kids from an acid bath just so mercenaries could gun them down.

I had no viable option except surrender—but maybe we could come out of this with some small advantage. Fortunately, Lilla stood right in front of me. Catching her eye, I whispered so quietly only she could hear me.

"I took your guns and forced you to help me."

Lilla gave a microscopic nod. Even better, when I dropped my blaster, she let her laser pistol fall, too. With my body between her and the mercenaries, none of them could know we'd both been armed. I gave her a smile and spread my arms wide.

"Sko, drop your gun."

The second Sko's gun hit the floor, Lilla bent and scooped up all three weapons. "She forced me to help her out. I'm not with her. Tell them, Milla."

"Don't shoot—she's my sister and a D Section manager." Milla sounded nervous. Considering my experiences with the Fringer crew, I didn't blame her. "She's got to be telling the truth."

I pretended to vent a frustrated sigh. "Yes, I made her come with me, but the rest of these kids are innocent, too."

"Do tell?" The captain sounded barely interested.

"Look, do what you want with me-"

"Oh, we will, Fed."

"But take the kids to the elevator and send them up to the inner world. If you don't, the AI will kill them. It already tried once."

Keeping my hands wide, I risked turning around. The Fringer captain and eight members of his crew stood in the doorway, blasters trained on Sko and me. Behind them, Mauris and Milla stood quietly watching the scene. Lilla, guns clutched to her chest, scurried between the men to join her sister.

"And why should I care?"

All the loathing the captain's comment brought out in me burned in my eyes. "Because they're *kids*. They're not involved in our little war. And not even *you* deserve to be thrown, alive, into an acid bath—which is what the AI tried to do."

The captain just raised an eyebrow, as if I'd suggested a place to go for lunch. To my relief, several members of his crew winced and exchanged uneasy glances.

"And like a good little Fed, you rushed in to save the boys and girls." The Fringer mercenary shook his head in mock admiration. "I got to say, Fed, you've been pretty busy since I saw you last. It didn't surprise me one bit to find out you've been as big a pain in the ass to my new friend Arktu as you've been to me."

Four robots rolled up from inside D Section and Arktu's voice boomed from all four. "Captain Dustin Smith, why have you not executed the prisoner?"

"I'll kill her when I'm good and ready to kill her. The same goes for the guy with her." Smith spoke with exaggerated patience. "Don't you want her to pay for all the trouble she's caused you?"

"You raise an excellent point, Captain Dustin Smith. Lock them away until we decide how best to eliminate them. Lock the workers in with them. I cannot spare robots to escort them to their promotion ceremony at this time."

"What promotion ceremony?" Smith asked.

"Remember the acid bath I told you about?" I asked.

As the robots turned and rolled away, Smith looked back and forth between the kids and robots. "Whatever."

Smith moved to one side, motioning his crew to let us pass between them. "Let's go. All of you."

Sko and I gathered the teenagers as close around us as possible. "It's okay, kids. I promise it's going to be okay."

Mauris, both of his blondes at his back once again, led us into D Section and around the workshop floor. Watching Lilla, I could tell she wanted to turn and look our way, but she kept facing forward. Smith and his crew took up positions around us, prodding any of the kids who moved too slowly for their tastes.

On the workshop floor, children fed piles of scrapped metal onto the conveyor belts, just as before. I smiled as I recognized where the metal came from.

"Hey Smith, have you taken a careful look around the workshop?"

"Don't need to, Fed. I've seen dozens of shops like this."

"I don't mean the machines." I gave Smith a bright smile. "Have you looked closely at the *scrap* they're feeding into the smelter?"

"Huh?" Smith looked puzzled at my unexpected comment, but his eyes wandered to the piles of metal standing next to the conveyers. "Hey, wait—is that-?"

"That used to be your ship's starboard engine, Smith."

"What the hell?"

"Come on, you didn't think the AI was going to let our ships just lay around in the docking bay, did you? Metal is a scarce resource on any ship—especially a generation ship like the *Ark 2*."

Smith fell into muttering and cursing, but nothing else changed. I hadn't expected anything else, but there had been a chance he'd run off and try to save the rest of his ship.

Moments later, Mauris directed us into an unlighted room barely big enough to hold Sko, the kids, and me. To my chagrin, Smith searched each of us for wristbands, taking all of mine and the one I'd given Kath. Before the door slid shut, I heard Smith ordering one of his men to stand guard. Then the door closed and plunged us into total darkness.

12

ESCAPE

"Nancy?" In the darkness, Kath's voice held rising terror. "I can't see you! Are you in here, Nancy?"

Kath's call to me broke the dam and the rest of the kids called out, too. Some began crying, afraid of being taken back to the hydroponics station. Some swore to make the robots kill them rather than let themselves be thrown into the acid pool. Every comment fed the terror already rising among my charges.

"*Nancy!*" Kath all but shrieked over the other voices.

Keeping my voice level and calm, I called, "Settle down, everyone. I'm right here, near the door."

I might as well have tried whispering over a tornado. My reasonable-toned voice never had a chance against two dozen scared kids. That's when Sko spoke up, taking a very different approach than I had.

"*Quiet!*" Sko yelled from right next to me, nearly bursting my eardrums and easily drowning out the teenagers' combined voices. To my amazement, every voice fell silent. In his normal voice, Sko said, "That's better. Now, keep your voices down and stop panicking. That just makes the situation worse—something we don't need right now. Is that clear?"

"Yes, sir," chorused the kids in chastened voices.

"Good. First things first—Nancy is right here next to me." Sko's hand groped for me in the dark, turning into an intimate grope when he laid it on my left breast. I barely kept from laughing at how quickly his hand jumped up to my shoulder and I staunchly resisted the sudden temptation to guide his hand back there. "Uh, say something Nancy."

"Something Nancy." That response is corny and older than dirt, but the situation required some kind of humor. The kids laughed as if they'd never heard the joke before. Trapped down here for years, slaving away for the AI, maybe they hadn't heard it.

"Second, remember that we've got help on the outside. If we can't get out on our own, Lilla will find a way to get us out—and she'll do that long before Arktu can gather any spare robots." Sko's voice held absolute confidence in our young ally, which had a further calming effect on the kids around us.

"And third," Sko continued, "we aren't as helpless as Arktu and those men think we are."

"What do you mean by that, Sko?" I asked

"Well, Captain, I've got a surprise for you in my pants."

If I thought the kids laughed hard at my little joke, they just about busted their guts laughing at Sko. Somehow, despite Sko's obvious lack of sexual experience, I got the idea Sko knew exactly what he was saying this time. While the kids roared, I felt Sko lean close and speak quietly into my ear.

"Teenagers respond well to a firm hand, my Captain, especially when they're scared. Act confident when you tell them what to do." Then Sko put something metallic and cool to the touch in my hand.

Unable to resist, I asked, "Why, Sko, is that a laser in your pants or are you just happy to see me?"

Laughter rose around us again as the kids closest to us overheard my question and passed it along to those farther away.

"It's a laser, of course," Sko replied. "I can't be happy to see you because it's too dark to see."

And that set the kids off again, though not quite as uproariously.

I heard sudden pounding on the door from outside and asked, "Gee, do you think all this laughter is bothering our guard?"

"Now that you're armed, perhaps you can end the man's irritation, my Captain. Can you open the door?" Sko asked.

"No, they took the piece of robotic arm when they took the wristbands. Too bad I didn't hide that in your pants, too." And then a question occurred to me. "I saw the men search you for wristbands. How did they miss the laser?"

"There aren't many men who are willing to search another man's...nether regions. Apparently, Smith's men are no different than most other men in that regard. With no way to open the door, though, how can we use it?"

"Our guard has given me an idea. Hey kids, yell at the top of your lungs if you're ready to get out of here."

The teenagers all yelled and yelled. Then one of them began banging on the door like it was a drum. Within seconds, every kid in the room pushed past me and joined in the drumming on the door and wall.

"Hey, move away from the door, kids. If it opens, I don't want anyone between me and the guard."

The drumming moved to the side, picked up speed, and settled into a pattern as all the kids got in synch with each other. I thought I heard banging from the other side of the door, but it was hard to tell over the racket from the drumming.

Then the miracle happened. A sliver of light appeared on the right side of the door and widened quickly. I squinted against the blinding light but never took my eyes from the doorway. The guard was against the far wall, his blaster pointed at the door, shouting something which got lost in the noise.

Without a bit of remorse, I raised the laser and shot him between the eyes.

As the Fringer guard slumped back against the wall, a neat hole burned into his forehead, Sko hurried out the door and caught the man's gun before it clattered to the floor. Then he hefted the man over his shoulder and carried him into our room. In the light shining through the open door, I saw the man wore three wristbands. I pulled all three of them—one red, one blue, and one white—from the man's wrist, then Sko dumped the body in a back corner. The kids shied away from the corpse, but still looked at it in morbid curiosity.

"D-did you have to kill him?" one boy asked quietly.

"Yes, she did," Sko responded as he stood after searching the body. "He would have shot my Captain without a second thought."

I slid the red band over my wrist and gave the other two to Sko. "He was left on guard to make sure all of you remained locked in this room until Arktu could take you back to the acid pool. He was no friend of ours."

At my mention of the acid pool, a shudder ran through the kids. I hated reminding them of that horror, but they had to remember the stakes we were fighting for.

"I know all of this is strange to you, but you've got to prepare yourself for what's to come." Sko traded guns with me and I admit it felt good having a blaster back in my hands. "Sko and I will have to shoot more people before this is over and some of you might even be forced to fight and kill, too. Those men won't hesitate to kill you, so let that knowledge guide your actions."

Some of the kids nodded, determination on their young faces. The rest looked less certain, but you never really know how combat affects people until they find themselves in a life or death situation.

"Sko and I will do our best to keep you out of the line of fire," I added. "With those men helping Arktu, my original plan of giving you data pads and sending you to warn your sections won't work anymore. That's why the first thing we do when we leave this room is get all of you kids up to the settled part of the ship and into a village."

"My Captain, we cannot just send these children to the surface and leave them on their own," Sko protested. "They might starve before they find a village."

"I know." I wrapped my arms around Sko and laid my head against his chest. "That's why I'm sending you with them."

Sko stiffened in my arms and several of the teenagers gasped in surprise.

"My Captain...Nancy, you cannot send me away from your side."

"I can and I must. Not only can you take these children to safety, you can get the blasters we left with your village. With the Fringer mercenaries down here, we're going to need them a lot more than the villagers are."

"So you want me to return to you after the children are safe?"

I looked up into Sko's eyes. "Always."

I lowered my eyes and pulled my arms back. Then Sko's strong, calloused hands gently caught my head between them and turned my face back toward his. His kiss was deep and loving and lingering and full of the promise of a future beyond anything I could have imagined a mere three days ago..

"And what will you do while I am gone, my Captain?"

"Sleep." Dream of you.

Taking a deep breath, I turned to face the kids and Sko let me go. "Okay, here's the plan. We're going to do our best to sneak back to the D Section door. Once there, Sko will take all of you back to the world within the ship. The world where you grew up."

"Will I get to see my parents?" Kath asked.

"Unless you're from Sko's village, not yet. Once we've taken care of Arktu, though, I promise to do everything in my power to reunite every child with his or her parents. Okay?" Heads nodded all around. "Good. Now, which of you kids is from D Section?"

When the boy and two girls raised their hands, I motioned them to come forward. "Can you find your way to the workshop floor from here?"

"I can," the boy said and one of the girls nodded.

"We're going to divide into two groups and I'm assigning one of you to each group. You're with me," I said to the boy, then turned to the girl. "I'm putting you with Sko, but don't you go flirting with him, you hear? He's mine."

The girl grinned and took Sko's arm. I quickly divided the kids into two groups and then sent him and his kids off into the hallway.

I turned to my guide once Sko's group was out of sight. "Do you know a different way to the workshop than the one she's taking?"

"Yes."

"Good. Take us by that route."

The boy headed off into the corridor, the others quietly trailing after him. Blaster at the ready, I fell in behind the last kid in line. As long as Smith hadn't assigned any of his men to patrol the hallways, I didn't expect any trouble. With the exception of Mauris, Milla, and Lilla, the kids working down here stuck to the direct path from the dormitory to the workshop and back again.

I felt a pang of worry for Lilla, hoping she didn't come to free us and, when she found the room empty except for the Fringer corpse, think I'd abandoned her. Finding her was my top priority once Sko and the kids were on their way. Unable to do anything else about Lilla at the moment, I put her out of my mind.

Ten minutes later, our guide led us around the activity on the workshop floor. I released a pent up breath I hadn't realized I was holding when we found Sko and the others waiting at the door. Sko and I shared a quick smile, then I motioned to the touch pad for the door. Sko touched one of his wristbands to the pad.

I winced as the door rumbled open, sounding louder than a spaceship lifting off to me. I kept an eye toward the workshop floor, but either the door opened so often no one noticed it anymore or the noise on the floor drowned out the rumbling of the doors. Either way, no one came to investigate.

As soon as the opening was wide enough, Sko started sending kids through the door. Within twenty seconds, the last kid slipped into the corridor. Giving me a smile and a wink, Sko followed the kids and touched the wristband to the pad in the corridor. The door reversed itself and I exchanged one last look with Sko before the door closed.

A sudden and thoroughly unfamiliar feeling of loneliness swept over me. Pushing it aside as best I could, I set off to find Lilla.

Not knowing where she might be, I climbed up onto the catwalk that ran around the outer wall of the workshop. If she was directing the work on the floor, her height and blonde hair ought to stand out among the other kids. Smith's men ought to stand out even more, so scouting from above served a dual purpose.

Seconds later, I gazed out at the sprawling workshop floor. As before, older children sliced large hunks of metal—from the remains of my ship and Smith's—into manageable pieces while younger children fed those pieces into the smelter. A few robots patrolled the floor, giving Arktu a view of the work.

I spotted Smith right in the middle of things, obviously shouting at one of the robots. All the while, Smith waved his arms wildly and pointed at what was left of one of his ship's engines. The robot didn't look at Smith or even respond to him, as best I could tell. It just rolled on with its patrol pattern. Finally, in apparent desperation, Smith yanked his blaster from its holster and waved it about in a threatening manner.

That got Arktu's attention. Every robot wheeled about and rolled toward Smith. The robots also obviously issued orders to the children, who all followed behind the robots. The kids with cutting torches kept those in hand while the empty-handed children picked up spanners, crowbars, or hammers.

In seconds, Smith and one of his men found themselves surrounded by as menacing a gang of children as I'd ever seen.

One robot rolled closer to Smith and I assume Arktu spoke to him through the robot. I couldn't hear anything the robot said, but I watched Smith's man pale visibly. Smith, on the other hand, reddened in anger but very slowly and carefully holstered his blaster. The robot spun about and the mob of children returned to their work.

As Smith stalked off toward the dormitory, I considered what I'd just seen. In my experience with the kids, they'd been excited to see Sko and me. I could imagine them reluctantly following Arktu's orders to hurt us, but never with such obvious menace as they'd shown to Smith. It looked like the idiot mercenary captain had shown the children the same winning personality he'd shown to me. And that meant I might be able to count on support from the children if I made any moves against Smith.

Tracking Smith's progress off of the floor, I spotted Lilla coming into the workshop from the dormitory. She gave Smith a hard look and walked wide around him before setting off toward the office. Smith said something to his man, who turned and trailed after Lilla.

An unsettling feeling grew in the pit of my stomach as I spotted the furtive glances the man gave the working children and their robot overseers. I all but ran down the stairs and vaulted the rail when I was halfway down. Cursing the need to stick to the shadows, I flitted around the edge of the work floor. Once I got around that, I sprinted between hulking, abandoned, and gutted machines toward the office at the back of the workshop. My fear ratcheted up several notches when I saw the blinds were drawn down, blocking any view into the office.

Pulling out my blaster, I skidded to a stop at the office door, slapped the red wristband against the contact plate, and slid through the opening as soon as it was wide enough. Smith must have left another of his men in the office, as the furtive one had his arms wrapped tightly around a struggling and crying Lilla while the other man pulled her pants off.

Tossing the pants aside, the man leered. "See, Hopkins, I told you she was a natural blonde."

Lilla kicked at the man before her, drawing a laugh from him and Hopkins. As the bastard dropped his own pants, I shot him in the back. The man arched his back and fell to the floor and Lilla and Hopkins looked my way. Hopkins' eyes bugged out at the sight of me. Lilla, bless her, stomped hard on Hopkins' foot.

Hopkins bellowed in pain and his grip loosened on Lilla. Instantly, she slid through his arms to the floor. Hopkins had just enough time to raise one hand in supplication before I blew a big hole through his head.

I barely registered the sound of the door closing itself behind me as I ran to Lilla. She sat on the floor, hugging herself and crying with deep, wracking sobs. I dropped to my knees and gathered her into my arms, stroking her hair as she released all of her terror. After a few minutes, she settled down enough for me to help her get dressed again. Not once did she look at the two dead men behind her.

"I prayed you'd come, Nancy, and you did!" Lilla flashed a brief smile at me before hugging me again. "Maybe the Captain really does watch over us."

"I'm just glad I got here in time, honey." I held her out at arm's length and looked her over. "Are you hurt?"

"Not on the outside." She gave me another quick smile. "And not on the inside so much. Not since you came."

"I wish I could just sit here and comfort you until you didn't hurt anywhere, Lilla, but I can't do that."

"I know Nancy. Just tell me what to do. I'll be okay."

"That's my brave girl." Still keeping an arm around her shoulder, I surveyed the room. "I need to get some more data pads and wristbands. Then we need to do something with these two bodies."

Lilla shuddered at that. "Why can't we just leave them here?"

"We could, but if we can get rid of the bodies it might put a little of the fear of God into Smith and his men."

"Fear of who?"

"God. For right now, just think of Him as my Captain."

I climbed over piled junk to reach the cabinets which held the data pads and wristbands. As before, I found rows of charged data pads and a box full of wristbands. Previously, I found and took two gold wristbands from the box. Now, I grabbed all of the colors I could find and, hoping to find more gold wristbands, checked the two cabinets I'd left alone the time before.

The first cabinet had some more wristbands, all red, and a lot of miscellaneous electronic and mechanical parts. The second cabinet held first aid kits and, hidden behind a pile of parts on the bottom shelf, a laser pistol, and a dozen power packs—all fully charged. Added to the two blasters the dead men had carried, Lilla and I were going to be very heavily armed.

I climbed back over the junk around the cabinet. The girl was staring at the bodies as if psyching herself up to help me drag them out of the office.

"Lilla, is there a float pallet nearby? If there is, I can take care of the bodies by myself."

"What?" She shook herself and forced her gaze away from the corpses. "Um, yeah. I think I can get one for you."

"Will you be okay going off on your own to get it?" I caught Lilla's gaze in mine. "I'll be happy to go with you if that's what you want."

"No, I'll be fine, Nancy. Besides, it's about time for shift change so there won't be anyone around to ask me questions."

I handed Lilla one of the blasters. "This has better stopping power than your laser. If any of Smith's men come toward you, shoot them."

She nodded and slipped out the door. I busied myself dragging the bodies out of the office. I decided to give Lilla another minute before I went looking for her. Right after I made that decision, she came into view pushing a float pallet.

Despite my insistence that I could manage, Lilla helped me

load the dead men onto the pallet. "Is anyone working the floor right now, Lilla?"

"Nope. It's shift change, like I thought."

"What about robots?"

"They escort the workers back to the dormitory and then bring the new shift in."

"Then I know exactly what to do with these bodies."

Two minutes later, Lilla and I hefted the dead men onto the conveyor belt. Within seconds, both corpses tumbled into the smelter.

"Now what?" Lilla asked.

"Now we both get some sleep and wait for Sko to return. Follow me."

I led Lilla out of D Section and back to the robot recharging room. Not willing to take the chance of letting Sko slip past me, I laid down right in front of the elevator door. Seconds later, I was sound asleep.

13

NOMADS

I gradually became aware of something moving next to me, as well as the murmur of voices. I lay on my left side with my head cradled in the crook of my arm. Someone was nestled up to me and my right arm was flung over a slender form. I cracked one eye open and found myself looking at the top of a head full of blonde hair. I almost gave into the temptation to close my eye and drift off again, but I heard the voice murmur again and forced myself to wake up.

"Lilla? Who are you talking to?"

"Hm?" she responded, something obviously distracting her attention.

I knocked playfully on the girl's head. "Ship to Lilla. Come in Lilla."

"Oh, Nancy, you're awake. I'm sorry, I didn't mean to crowd you." Lilla stiffened and tried to roll away from me, but I tightened my arm and held her in place.

"You're not crowding me, Lilla, though I'm pretty sure you weren't snuggled up this close when I fell asleep."

"I felt...That is, I..." The girl trailed off, unsure of what to say.

"Were you scared or lonely or just cold?"

"Yes," she answered in a small voice. "I know I'm too old for that, but-"

"Stop right there, young lady. You can never be too old to draw comfort from another person." I gave her a little squeeze. "Are you feeling better or do you want to stay where you are for a bit longer?"

I felt the girl's body relax. "I want to stay here for a little longer. I feel safe next to you."

"That's fine." I propped my head up on my hand. "You know, when I woke up I could have sworn I heard you talking to someone."

"That was me asking one of those data pad things to show me maps of the ship."

"*What?*" Lilla jumped in my arm, obviously startled by my exclamation. "Shhh. Relax, Lilla. I didn't mean to startle you."

The girl settled a bit though remained tense. "You're not mad at me?"

"Are you kidding? I'm thrilled. I want you to show me how you got the pad to work by voice command."

"Well, I woke up a while ago. I knew you needed your sleep, so I stayed still and quiet so I wouldn't wake you up. But that got boring, so I started playing around with one of the data pads. You know, it all starts to make sense once you play around with it for a while."

Even without a technological background, Lilla was no different than kids across the galaxy. Hand them an interesting gadget, show them just enough to get them started using it, and the next thing you know they've figured out how to do things the gadget's designers didn't even know the gadget could do. At my request, she taught me everything she'd figured out—which was a lot.

Eventually, I could call up the ship's maps without going through the work order screen and learned how to enable voice commands. Feeling my excitement building, I held the pad before me and said, "Display the bridge."

The screen blinked and a new map displayed, with a highlighted area that had to be the *Ark 2's* command center. Now for the big test. "Display the route from my location to the bridge."

The map automatically zoomed out and out and out, eventually overlaying a green line connecting what must be our location with the bridge.

"That looks like a long way, Nancy," Lilla said, looking at the map with me.

"Yeah, it sure does." It was time to try a new command. "Display the total distance of the route from my location to the bridge."

Even when I was prepared for the answer, I gasped when it appeared.

Lilla looked at me with concern and asked, "Is fifty-three, uh, what's the word?"

"Kilometers."

"Is fifty-three kilometers a long way?"

I nodded. "It's more than half the length of the ship. God only knows what Arktu can throw at us along such a long journey."

"But we're going to go there and...do whatever it is you do to stop Arktu, right?"

"Absolutely, Lilla, though I can't go until Sko gets back."

"Of course not!" Lilla appeared shocked I even felt the need to say that. "I can go, too, right? I don't want to stay in D Section."

"I'll tell you what, if I can't find a way to get you to Sko's village then you can come with us. How's that sound?"

"Okay, I guess."

Any reply I had fled from my mind as I heard the elevator machinery come to life. Lilla, who'd never heard the sound before, spun and looked at the closed elevator door in alarm.

"That's just the machine that took Sko up to the inner ship, Lilla. It probably means Sko is on his way back down here now."

The girl visibly relaxed and grinned. "Are you going to give him a big kiss?"

"We'll see what happens when Sko gets down here." I shook my head in mock disapproval at the question. "Meanwhile, let's play it safe and get out of sight until we're sure it really *is* Sko in the elevator."

Remembering where Sko and I hid when we first came down here, I led Lilla to the same robot. After I assured her the robot couldn't move even if it wanted to, we slid around the edge of the robot and took up a position on the robot's treads.

Five minutes later, the elevator ground to a halt. Light spilled into the room as the doors slid open. Along with the light came the sound of hushed conversations. Then three men, all armed with bows, stepped out of the elevator. Once they gave the 'all clear' signal, more men piled out of the elevator. Soon, a good twenty of them milled about in the room—and none of them were Sko.

Lilla tapped my shoulder as I stared at the men who'd come in the elevator. Turning to her, I met a wide-eyed, concerned stare barely visible in the dim light.

With exaggerated care, she mouthed, "Where's Sko?"

I shrugged, put a finger to my lips, and turned back to watching the men. They kept a nervous eye on all the robots surrounding them, no doubt remembering run-ins they'd had with culling patrols. The men couldn't know I'd reversed the robot charging mechanism and discharged the robots' batteries, though I found myself wishing they did. Too many eyes were roaming the robot alcoves for me to feel comfortable about our hiding place.

"The villager said the door was across from the moving room," the obvious leader announced. "Quit milling around like a gaggle of women and check it out."

With reluctance, the men tore their eyes from the robots and headed for the door. The leader tapped something on the touchpad and the door slid open. In the light from the hallway, I recognized a red wristband—the same color as the one I'd given Sko. The sight swept away any doubt I'd had as to the identity of the 'villager' the leader mentioned.

The leader signaled the men through the door, but another man spoke up first. "Marn, should we leave a guard?"

Marn, the leader, paused and looked back at the elevator, considering the question. I bent all of my non-existent mental powers toward convincing Marn that no guard was required.

After a few interminable heartbeats, Marn shook his head. "No, the moving room isn't going anywhere and we'll need every man to take back our children."

Quietly sighing with relief, I watched the last of the men exit the room. Seconds later, the door slid quietly shut.

"Who were those men, Nancy?" Lilla asked. "I don't think they're part of Sko's village."

"Nomads. Sko and I found a tribe of them outside the elevator the first time we tried to return to the village." I motioned for Lilla to follow me out of our hiding place. "I didn't think they'd wait this long, otherwise I'd never have sent Sko and the other kids to the village."

"D-do you think they killed Sko?"

Lilla's lip trembled as she asked the question. I gave her shoulder a squeeze. "I don't know, Lilla." God, I pray not. I led her into the elevator. "There's only one way to find out."

Lilla followed me without hesitation, though not without thought. "Will we find more nomads when we get off the elevator?"

I patted my blaster as I keyed the elevator to ascend. "If we do, I'm ready for them."

Patting her own blaster, Lilla flashed a predatory smile. "You and me both, Nancy."

The ride up only took a few minutes, but it felt like an eternity. Finally, the elevator slowed. Drawing our blasters, Lilla and I took up positions next to the door. I put myself in the most direct line of fire, with Lilla to the side where she'd only be revealed after the door opened a few feet.

The elevator stopped and the door slid open with a quiet hiss. The smells of nature wafted in on the breeze as I blinked into bright, mid-afternoon simulated sunlight. I didn't see a single person, but Lilla waved for my attention and pointed out and to the left. I leaned out of the elevator and looked where she was pointing.

A young man, probably no older than Lilla, faced the rocks not more than four meters away. His pants were loose around his waist and I heard the unmistakable sound of water splashing against rock. I motioned for Lilla to follow me, noting her thus-far successful attempts to smother a case of the giggles.

The stream of water cut off abruptly when I placed the blaster against the back of the boy's neck. "Put your hands up, son."

He did as instructed and, without a hand holding them up, his pants dropped down around his ankles. That was too much for Lilla, who burst into a fit of giggles. The boy looked over his shoulder, his face reddening.

"Behave," I admonished Lilla. To the boy, I added, "Pull up your pants, son."

While the boy covered himself, I looked over my shoulder. "Lilla, take a quick look around and see if you can find evidence of a camp. Stay in clear sight of me, though, and come right back to me if you see anything."

Lilla nodded and set off to do my bidding. By then, the boy was done with his pants and gauging the distance to his bow.

"Don't even think of going for the bow. I don't want to shoot you, but I will if I have to." The boy showed uncommonly good sense and stopped eying his weapon. "What's your name?"

"Raal."

"My name is Nancy and the giggle box is Lilla. Believe me when I say I really don't want to hurt you. I just want to find my friend and move on out of here."

"Is your friend a big villager?"

"Yes. Is he okay? Where can I find him?"

About then, Lilla dashed back to me. "I found Sko. He's tied to a tree over that way."

"Were there any other guards?" I asked, unable to hide my relief.

"There's a bunch of women, some old men, and boys even younger than this guy," Lilla jerked a thumb at Raal.

"Good job, Lilla." Motioning to the boy, I said, "Lead the way, Raal. And don't shout or think about running away. I can blow your leg off with this weapon before you get three feet."

"I know. Marn tested one after we took it off of the villager. It knocked down the tree Marn shot at."

I nodded for the boy to start walking and he did, keeping his hands up. "Lilla, get his bow."

A moment later, we walked into the nomad camp and, when they spotted us, brought everything to a standstill. Sko smiled happily, especially when I sent Lilla over to cut him free. Meanwhile, an older woman stalked up to Raal and slapped him soundly on the face.

"Stupid boy! You let a *woman* capture you?"

"She's got one of those blast things like the villager had," Raal told her. "And she came out of the door in the rock. It didn't make any sound and Marn told me not to worry about watching it since he'd be in control wherever they went."

I snorted a harsh laugh at that. I couldn't help myself.

The woman turned her glare on me. "What do you find so funny, village bitch?"

"My, aren't you the charming one?" Being somewhat of a professional in the glaring business, I glared at the woman the way I glared at fresh recruits. "What I find funny is the idea that Marn and his men are going to be in control of anything down there. If you're very lucky, they'll quickly figure out they can't control anything down there and run back up here with their tails between their legs. If you're not so lucky, they're already dead."

A fluttering of talk burst out behind the woman. She spun and turned her glare on the others in the camp. "What makes you think this villager knows anything? Shut up and trust Marn to get our children and bring them and our men back to us—just like he always does."

I joined Lilla and Sko at the edge of the camp. "I honestly hope Marn does that because no child deserves to be down there. Meanwhile, I've got business of my own to attend to. Don't try following us. My friend knows this area and we've all got the blasting weapons."

With that, Sko, Lilla, and I turned and headed into the woods.

14

LILLA IS A VERY SMART GIRL

"I didn't see the children we saved from the acid bath anywhere in the camp, Sko." I tried to sound calm as I broached the subject, but I didn't even fool myself. "Did you get them safely to your village?"

"Yes, my Captain." Sko's large hand enveloped mine as we walked. "The nomads caught me on my way back."

I breathed a sigh of relief. "That's one thing less to worry about, though now I've got to put Marn and his nomad warriors on my worry list in place of those kids."

"Why are you worried about him?" Lilla asked.

"I'm not so much worried for him as for the problems he's going to cause for us." With my free hand, I massaged my temples. "After Marn's attack, Arktu will have the whole section on alert and will summon more robots to patrol the area. It's going to make it almost impossible for us to slip past Arktu unnoticed. And it won't take Arktu long to figure out where we're going and set up ambushes along the way."

As familiar as Lilla was with Arktu's methods, I was surprised she hadn't figured this out on her own. Perhaps she was still reeling after her near rape by two of Smith's men or maybe the whole situation was overwhelming her. Whatever the reason, I wasn't going to voice my surprise. All things considered, she deserved time to come to grips with it all.

Lilla looked at me in surprise. "You're planning to go back down in the elevator and follow the route to the command place?"

"The bridge. Yes."

"Why, Nancy?"

Maybe Lilla was suffering more than I thought. "Because I've got to get to the bridge to shut down Arktu, honey."

"Yeah, I know *that*." Damned if the girl didn't roll her eyes at me like I was stupid or something. Then Lilla raised the data pad she'd been playing around with. "Display a map of our location and the shortest route to the bridge."

She turned the pad so I could see the display. A wilderness map covered three-quarters of the screen, with the leftmost quarter showing a map of corridors. A red line traced across the wilderness to an arrow pointing both up and down—no doubt an elevator. From there, the red line traced through corridors to the bridge.

Lilla pointed toward one end of the ship. "It looks like we go that way."

"I'll be damned. I never even thought of this approach." Obviously, the girl standing before me wasn't the one turned stupid by everything we'd been through. I grinned at Lilla. "Smart thinking, young lady. We'll make an officer out of you yet."

Lilla flushed with pride at the compliment. Meanwhile, Sko leaned in close to study the pad's display screen.

"This is amazing, Lilla, but it's very small and hard to see," he said.

"Just say 'zoom in on my location' and it'll get bigger."

Sko took the pad from me and repeated Lilla's words. His eyebrows arched in surprise and the spark of interest ignited in his eyes. Looking at Lilla, he said, "You must teach me how to use this thing."

"Lessons while we walk, people," I said. "We've only got a few hours of light left and I don't want to be near the nomad camp when it gets dark."

It didn't take long for Lilla to show Sko how to control the pad. Soon, he was scrolling around the map, planning our path and muttering about details and the best way to avoid nomad pursuit. As a result, we left the direct route shown on the pad and waded through shallow streams, hiked across rock-strewn fields hopping from rock to rock, and generally did other stuff to utterly exhaust a rocket jockey like me. Sko, on the other hand, looked as if he could keep this pace up forever. During one break, while I lay gasping on the ground, he even slipped off and shot a couple of rabbits for dinner.

Finally, as dusk settled across the ship, Sko called a halt. "I've camped here many times on hunting trips. There aren't any big predators in the area, there's fresh water for drinking, and even a warm pool beyond those bushes."

Sko cleaned the rabbits while Lilla and I gathered dry wood. Once Sko had a smokeless fire burning and rabbits cooking, I plucked at the sweat stained jumpsuit I'd been wearing for three days.

"So I can take a bath and wash my clothes?"

Sko didn't quite meet my eyes. "Yes, my Captain. It's one reason I chose this place for our camp."

"You're my hero." I rose up on the balls of my feet and kissed his cheek. Lowering myself, I let my hand trace down Sko's arm, clasped his hand, and then let it fall as I turned toward the bushes. "I'll just be over there. In the pool. Bathing."

Sko watched me go. Lilla watched Sko watch me go. Both were still watching when I pushed between the bushes and lost sight of them.

A small pool, maybe eight meters across, lay before me. The ground around it was sandy, as was the bottom of the pool. Peeling off my sticky jumpsuit, I wondered how something as perfect as this pool could have formed. Then I remembered I was on a generation ship, not in a real wilderness. Millennia ago, some nature lover on the design staff put this pool here for just this reason.

The water was pleasantly cool on my body as I waded into it up to my thighs. I cupped some water and rubbed it on my face. Then I dove in, swam a short way, and then surfaced, treading water.

As I shook wet hair out of my eyes, I heard a sound behind me. I turned to see Sko emerge from the bushes.

"Lilla says I'm an idiot and that you wanted me to come with you," he said, hands tentatively reaching for the ties fastening his shirt.

I smiled. "Lilla is a *very* smart girl."

When Sko and I pushed back through the bushes and back into our camp, Lilla sat before the small fire gnawing on some of the cooked rabbit. Her eyes danced in the flickering firelight and she wore a smugly satisfied expression.

"Told you she wanted you to go with her," she said to Sko around a mouthful of rabbit. She switched her gaze to me. "Left to yourselves, the two of you would still be trying to figure out how you felt about each other."

"Yes, Lilla, you're a genius." I reached for a spit holding one of the rabbits and met the girl's eyes. "Now shut up."

A delighted laugh rose from deep within Lilla. She leaned back and began rolling back and forth cackling like an evil witch in a fairy tale. Sko looked at me, shrugged, and pulled a rabbit haunch off the spit. For some reason, the girl found that even more hilarious and laughed all the harder.

Eventually, our stomachs full and Lilla laughed out, I offered to watch over the girl while she bathed. For some reason, this set off another round of giggles, but Lilla took me up on the offer. While we were at the pool, Sko used the data pad's map to plan our route for the next day. Then, with Sko and me alternating on watch, we got some sleep.

We made an early start the next morning, setting off just past first light. As before, Sko led us through the most difficult terrain in an effort to make sure no one from the nomad camp could pick up our trail. Long before lunch, I was covered in sweat and my legs burned with the unaccustomed exertion. When we finally stopped for lunch next to a stream, I simply collapsed to the ground and lay there gasping.

With disgusting grace and an apparent lack of effort, Sko settled to his knees next to me. His strong hands kneaded my thighs and calves, working the tightness and knots from the muscles. Meanwhile, Lilla pulled out leftover rabbit and got fresh water from the stream.

Watching the two of them moving effortlessly, I glared white-hot death at them. "You realize that I hate both of you right now."

Instead of burning to a crisp under my death gaze, Sko and Lilla just laughed. It sounded all innocent, but I felt sure both laughs held sadistic undertones. Smiling, Lilla casually sank to her knees opposite Sko, lifted my head, and gave me a drink of cool, wonderful water. Then she popped a piece of rabbit meat into my mouth.

Patting my head, she said, "Remember to chew it up really good before you swallow, Nancy."

Growling, I sat up and took the rabbit and water from Lilla and started feeding myself. When I did, Sko stopped massaging my legs and reached for some of the rabbit.

"Did I tell you that you could stop, Sko?" I demanded.

"No, my Captain," Sko said through a wide grin, "but I'm sure even you recognize that your devoted servants must maintain their strength so they can serve you to the best of their ability."

I gave a magnanimous wave of my hand, allowing him to continue eating. "Aren't we far enough from the nomads that we can stop trying to hide our trail? I mean, they don't know we came this way and probably have a lot better things to do than come after us. And that's assuming Marn didn't get all of his men killed storming the dormitory armed with bows and arrows."

"They also had the blaster and laser Marn took from me," Sko added.

"Okay, so they probably did some damage when they first stormed into the dormitory but once Smith and his people joined the fight, things probably went from bad to worse for Marn very quickly."

"You make a compelling argument, my Captain. After this break, I will take easier and more direct routes to the elevator we're looking for."

Sko proved true to his word and my whole body was grateful. Even taking the easier path, I didn't complain when Sko found another perfect spot to camp and called an early halt to our march.

As with the previous night's camp, this one was designed to be the perfect camping spot. Shade trees surrounded a flat, grassy area just right for sleeping. Another pool, this time with a smooth, rocky bottom, was separated from the main camp by a small mound topped with short evergreen trees.

I desperately wanted nothing more than to strip off my sweaty clothes and relax in the pool with Sko, but Lilla was just as grimy as I was and didn't deserve to wait around for the adults to finish... relaxing. "You can have the first bath, young lady. Come on, I'll keep watch while you get cleaned up."

Lilla crossed her arms, canted her hips, and gave me a cross look. "Why do *you* get Sko both nights? Isn't it *my* turn to 'relax' with him?"

My mouth fell open. "Uh, honey, it's...Um..."

At the same time, Sko's eyes bugged out and his face turned bright crimson. "Lilla, that's uh...You see, um..."

Lilla suddenly dissolved into a fit of laughter and gasped, "That...was...perfect! You should see your faces."

I did my best to glare at the girl and failed miserably. "You almost gave Sko a heart attack, Lilla."

Sko chimed in, grinning, "And I don't believe I've ever seen Nancy at such a loss for words. You should be ashamed of yourself."

Smiling broadly, Lilla sashayed toward the pool. Just before slipping between the trees, she looked over her shoulder in a coquettish manner. "You'll never know what you missed, Sko."

As I headed after her, Sko muttered, "May the Captain watch over the body and soul of the young man who captures that girl's heart."

I laughed. "Yes, that young man will have his hands full with Lilla—much to his delight."

"I have no doubt of that, my Captain."

By the time Lilla finished in the pool, Sko had a couple of fresh-caught birds roasting over a fire. Lilla settled down next to the fire and gave Sko and me an imperious wave.

"Go bathe and...whatever."

To my surprise, Sko not only did not blush, he scooped me up in his arms and carried me toward the pool. "Well, if you *insist*, Lilla."

Much later and much relaxed, Sko and I returned to the camp fire. Slipping through the trees, we both stopped short at the scene before us.

Lilla sat beside the fire, holding a partially eaten wing in one hand. Her other hand held her blaster trained on Raal, the young man from the nomad camp.

15

A NEW ALLY

"Look what I found skulking around our camp!" Lilla exclaimed brightly. She turned a glare on the boy at the business end of her blaster. "Of course, he might have snuck up and captured *me* if he hadn't found certain...sounds...coming from the pool so interesting."

Sko and I exchanged startled looks, our cheeks reddening at the thought of what Raal saw. Lilla laughed and waved the hand holding the bird wing in a placating manner.

"Don't worry, Raal stepped on a stick long before he could get a look through the trees. He didn't see you two." The blonde girl grinned mischievously around another bite of bird wing. "But we both sure heard plenty. It sounded like you two *relaxed* three or four times. Feeling better, are we?"

I felt it was time to regain control of the conversation. "That's enough of that, young lady. You do realize it's impolite to listen in to other people's private...conversation."

It was a lame finish to a lame attempt to chastise Lilla and she knew it. "I could have stuck my fingers in my ears and sung '*la la la la la'* but then sneaky-boy could have run off." The girl heaved a dramatic sigh. "So, Raal and I had no choice but to be impolite." Lilla shifted her amused gaze back to the boy. "Nancy, your, um, *discussion* with Sko had a really interesting effect on Raal—despite having a blaster trained on him."

Raal's blushed furiously and looked down, drawing a giggle from Lilla.

"Lilla!" Sko's voice cracked like a whip. "That is enough. A little teasing and joking is one thing, but you have gone far beyond that. Stop this foolishness at once."

Lilla's eyes flew wide and her jaw dropped open. I found myself gaping at Sko, too.

"I'm sorry, Sko," Lilla said, dropping her eyes to the fire before her. "I didn't mean anything by it."

"I know you didn't, Lilla." Sko's tone softened but remained reproachful. "You have a good heart, but sometimes you get too caught up with amusing yourself and don't think of the feelings of those around you. Do you understand?"

Lilla nodded her head. "I'll try not to do it again."

"Good." Sko smiled warmly at the girl. "Once you finish your apologies, we won't speak of this incident again."

Lilla lifted her head and solemnly met my gaze. "I'm sorry I embarrassed you, Nancy. You know I'd never hurt you on purpose."

I also met Lilla's apology with a smile. "You're forgiven."

A relieved smile spread across Lilla's face and she pointed us to the roasting bird. "Grab something to eat. It's really good."

I started forward, only to find Sko holding me back. He looked back and forth between Lilla and Raal, his meaning clear.

"You want me to apologize to *him*?" Lilla asked, incredulous.

"You embarrassed him, as well," Sko replied, sternness creeping back into his voice.

"But he followed us and snuck up on us. Why should I be polite to him?"

"Did you ask him *why* he followed us?"

"Um, no."

Sko released my hand, crossed his arms, and gave Lilla a meaningful look.

Lilla looked at Raal. "Sorry I embarrassed you."

The boy met her gaze briefly before quickly looking away. "That's okay. Boys joke like that all the time."

"There, that wasn't so hard, was it?" Sko asked, not expecting an answer.

He and I settled before the fire. Sko pulled one of the skewers off the fire and offered some meat to me. He surprised Raal by giving him some before pulling a breast off for himself. Before he could take a bite, Lilla leaned into him and wrapped her arms around his neck. She gave him a quick kiss on the cheek then rested her head on his chest.

Sko's eyebrows rose in surprise, but he wrapped an arm around the girl and gave her a hug. "What was that for, Lilla?"

"You reminded me of my father. I haven't thought about him in a long, long time but all of a sudden I miss him terribly."

"Don't you worry," Sko said, gently kissing her blonde head. "Once Nancy gets this Arktu thing settled, we will find your village and your parents. You and Milla, both."

"Um, sir?" Raal spoke up.

All three of us turned our attention to the boy and Sko asked, "Yes, Raal?"

"That's why I came looking for you. Because of that Arktu person, I mean—not about returning Lilla to her village." Raal smiled at Lilla in the friendly manner boys his age smile at pretty girls Lilla's age. "Not that I wouldn't do everything I could to return her to her village, sir, because I would. Or I'd help you return her."

Lilla stared at the boy as if seeing him for the first time. Sko merely nodded as if Raal's statement was nothing unexpected, then said, "But back to Arktu?"

Raal tore his gaze from Lilla and looked back and forth between Sko and me. "Arktu knows where you're going and Marn is taking the men from our camp to capture you for Arktu."

"Wait a minute," I interrupted, "are you saying Marn is working with Arktu now? How is that even possible?"

"I don't know all of it because I was being punished for getting caught by you. But I overheard a lot of the talk. Marn led the men to attack Arktu and get back the children the servants took a few days ago. Instead of fighting, Arktu traded the children for Marn's help capturing you three." Raal looked at me before looking at the ground as if ashamed of this next bit. "You were nice to me when you caught me outside the moving room. I won't help you fight my people, but I don't want you turned over to Arktu and the dirty guy who works with him."

"What dirty guy?" I asked, truly puzzled.

"Maybe I'm getting his name wrong, but Marn called him 'dirt in smith' or something like that."

I couldn't help but laugh at that and made a mental note to try it out on Smith if I ever saw him again. "You mean *Dust*in Smith."

Raal nodded, "Yeah, that's it. Anyway, Marn and the men ran ahead to catch you at the door to another moving room. I wasn't allowed to go, but snuck out and followed. I lost Marn's trail, but then I picked yours up a few hours ago."

Right after I asked Sko to stop taking the hard route. And a good thing, too, if Raal's story was true. We'd have walked right into Marn's ambush otherwise.

Something suddenly occurred to me. "Wait, how does Arktu know where we want to go?"

"I couldn't really follow that part." Raal's face screwed up as he tried to remember something. "Marn said it had something to do with a quilt. Even he wasn't sure about it."

"A quilt?" I turned a look of complete incomprehension toward Sko. "That doesn't make any sense."

Lilla suddenly sat up in excitement. "Oh! Did they say anything about reading a map on the quilt?"

Raal nodded.

Lilla bounced in excitement. "Nancy, quilts are *padded*. Arktu meant the data pad but Marn doesn't know what that is."

Oh, hell, Arktu was monitoring the data pad and read the map Lilla pulled up on the pad. I slapped my forehead, then another idea hit me. "But why doesn't Arktu track the data pad and just send Marn right to us?"

"We don't know what that means, my Captain," Sko said.

"The explanation is complicated, but Arktu should be able to use machines to find the data pad we're using. Then he could just send Marn straight to us and save all of this other trouble." I looked up to gaze off into space and once again found myself suffering vertigo as I stared at the settled area halfway around the cylinder of the ship. "Maybe Arktu let the sensors in this part of the ship fall into disrepair because he didn't want to waste resources fixing something he never used?"

I looked back at my companions. "Whatever the reason, we've still got big problems. I don't know how we're going to get to the elevator—that's the moving room to you, Raal."

"That's why I came looking for the three of you," Raal said. "I can help you get to it."

"Why would you help us against your own people?" Sko asked.

Raal glanced at Sko before shifting his gaze to me. "Like I told you, she was nice to me when she didn't have to be."

I waited for Sko to say something like 'oh yeah' and get on with asking what Raal's plan was. Instead, Sko stayed silent and stared intently at the boy. Raal, meanwhile, tried looking everywhere but at Sko. In the end, Sko's unwavering attention dragged the boy's eyes back to meet his gaze.

"What?" Raal demanded.

"I'm waiting for you to tell me the real reason you followed us," Sko replied. "A typical teenage boy doesn't trail after a woman the

Captain's age simply because she didn't kill him when she caught him with his pants down."

"Maybe I'm not typical," Raal protested. "And maybe I don't trust that Dustin guy and think you need to shoot him with your blast thing, because that will be best for my people."

Sko nodded once. "I believe that's part of it."

"That seems like more than enough to me," I said. "And I think it shows uncommonly good sense on Raal's part to not trust Smith."

"Yes, but if that's the main reason he's here, Raal can help the nomads best by making sure we get captured. Even if Smith proves untrustworthy, by the time he finishes dealing with us the nomads will have left this part of the ship and never return to it." Sko shook his head slowly. "If those are Raal's only reasons for following us, I cannot risk trusting him. He will do what is best for the nomads, not what is best for us."

I sighed, realizing that Sko was probably right. I wanted to get to the bridge before Arktu sent more kids to the acid bath and had let that desire get in the way of my better judgment. "Point taken, Sko."

In a sudden rush, Raal blurted, "I followed you so I could see Lilla again."

"What?" Lilla and I both asked.

Out of the corner of my eye, I saw a satisfied smile spread across Sko's face.

"I've never met a girl who wasn't part of my tribe before," Raal muttered, looking at the ground before him. "None of the girls in the tribe are my age. And even though she was laughing at me, I liked Lilla's laugh." Raal's voice dropped even lower. "And she's really pretty, too."

I had believed the boy's insistence that he would help get Lilla back to her family was nothing more than a clumsy attempt to impress Sko. Watching Raal watching Lilla for her reaction to his confession, I realized just how unobservant I'd been of late. Perhaps I'd missed the clues because Lilla had also missed the clues. Apparently I am not the only one who can spot how others feel about each other without being able to spot how others feel about me.

"You came all this way just to see *me* again?" she asked, staring at Raal in surprise and wonder.

"Well, yeah," Raal replied, as if traipsing across forty kilometers of wilderness in the hopes of seeing Lilla again was a no-brainer. Based on Lilla's responding smile, the honest simplicity of his answer obviously pleased her mightily.

"You never lost Marn's trail, did you boy?" Sko asked.

"Of course not," Raal scoffed. "What kind of tracker loses the trail of two dozen warriors who aren't bothering to hide their path? I was looking for you all along."

"And you'd never do anything to hurt Lilla?" Sko added, his tone intensifying.

"No!"

"Two of Smith's men have already tried to force themselves on Lilla," Sko continued. "If she falls into their hands again..."

"They'll have to kill me to get to her." Raal turned to Lilla. "And if you see the men who tried to— to— well, they're dead men when I see them!"

"Nancy already killed them," Sko told him. "But now I believe that you will do all in your power to help us."

I turned a surprised look on Sko. "All it takes is a confessed infatuation with Lilla to win your trust?"

"In this instance, yes." Sko waved a hand toward Raal. "Do you believe what he just told us?"

I nodded. "I do."

"When a man joins you to fight *against* someone, he may betray you if it will ensure his victory." Raal bristled at that, but Sko waved him down. "But a man who fights to *protect* one of your own will never betray you because betrayal may endanger the very person the man fights to protect."

"If Sko is happy, I'm happy." I looked at Raal, who was grinning at Lilla. "Welcome to the team, Raal. So, what's your plan for helping us get past Marn and his men?""

"I will lead you around the men—I know how Marn will arrange them—to a place where you can see the moving room. Then double back and come up from the direction he expects you to come from. I'll tell him you've stopped for the day and then lead him away from the moving room."

"And what will happen to you when Marn finds out you've tricked him?" Sko asked.

"He'll probably beat me and maybe send me into exile."

"But what if he kills you?" Lilla gasped. "We can't let him do that, Nancy."

"I agree," I said, then stared off into the distance for a few seconds. "Lilla, find out where the next closest elevator down into the ship is. Maybe we can just avoid Marn completely. Raal, did Smith give Marn any devices? A pad like the one Lilla has or some way to communicate with Smith?"

"I don't think so. Smith used a pad to show Marn where the... elevator...is. This is all part of our tribe's territory. Once Smith showed it to Marn and explained the map thing, Marn knew exactly where to go."

"Good. Arktu is probably monitoring our pads and will know we're trying for another elevator. Maybe Smith and his men will try to intercept us, but Marn won't know where we went."

Lilla pulled a pad out of its case and reached for the power button. Sko reached over and covered the button with his hand.

"Wait until morning, Lilla. We need sleep and I don't want to give Arktu all night to plan for our new destination."

I dropped my head into my hands. "Good God, I should have thought of that."

"You're tired and you can't think of everything, my Captain,"

Sko said, putting an arm around me. "Finish eating and then get some sleep. Raal and I will keep watch tonight."

I nodded my head wearily and did exactly as Sko suggested. I finished eating and lay down facing away from the fire. I just managed to curl an arm under my head before sleep claimed me.

Sko shook me gently, drawing me into wakefulness. I smiled lazily, hanging onto the last vestiges of sleep for just a moment more, and pulled Sko down into a long, slow kiss good morning.

"I'll deliver on the promise in that kiss tonight, once we've taken care of Arktu," I murmured as our lips parted.

"And I'll hold you to your promise, my Captain."

Sko pulled me up into a sitting position and I looked around. Lilla and Raal sat a few meters away, fiercely not watching Sko and me. Lilla pretended to play with the data pad and Raal pretended to watch. I found their attempts to give Sko and me the illusion of privacy touching and not a little funny.

Sko handed me a cold bird wing as I called to the teenagers. "Okay, you two can stop pretending to play with the data pad. Lilla, it's time to find out if there's another elevator we can take. Start off with a range of ten kilometers from the elevator."

Lilla issued the command to the data pad. A couple of seconds later, she grinned and spun the pad around so we could see it. "Got one—maybe nine kilometers past the first elevator, if I'm reading this right. Let me check the best path." Lilla turned the pad back to face herself. "Display the shortest path from our current location to the new elevator."

A puzzled look came over Lilla's face. "That can't be right."

"What is it, Lilla?" Sko asked.

The girl turned the pad so we could see the screen and pointed to a crooked, winding path to the newly located elevator. "It says the shortest path to the elevator is twenty-two kilometers."

It took us a few minutes to finally coax the reason for the circuitous route out of the data pad, but the path made perfect sense once we did. The elevator entrance was atop a fifty meter tall cliff. The long route traded distance for a safe ascent.

I took the pad from Lilla. "Display the route from the new elevator to the bridge." I studied the new addition for a moment. "I think this will do. It'll take us longer to get to the elevator, but the new elevator opens closer to the bridge than the original one. On top of that, the path takes us straight through officer territory."

All three of my companions turned uncomprehending looks my way and I realized they'd have no idea what 'officer territory' meant. "That's where officers live and sleep. With a little luck maybe we can even find the captain's cabin and search it. It's a long shot, but we might find a log book or journal explaining what happened."

A look of awe came over Raal's face. "Do you mean *the* Captain?"

I'd gotten so used to Sko and Lilla, I'd forgotten we'd never really explained what was going on to Raal. "Yes, more or less. Tell you what, I'll explain as we walk."

And I did just that. Raal listened attentively for a while before drifting back to walk with Lilla and discuss what I'd told him. After ten to fifteen minutes spent absorbing and discussing my revelations, Raal returned with questions for me. This cycle went on for most of the morning before Raal decided he'd had enough for one day.

As with Sko and Lilla, the concept of anything existing beyond the ship was hardest for Raal to wrap his head around. Unlike those two, he came up with a new approach to visualization.

Raal walked silently next to Lilla for a few minutes before asking, "Can that pad show you what it looks like outside the ship?"

Overhearing this comment, Sko stopped for a rest and we all gathered around Lilla and the data pad. I detected a slight tremor in her voice as Lilla said, "Display a view outside of the ship."

A second later, a star field replaced the map to the elevator. The odd asteroid spun past, otherwise it looked pretty much the same as when my starfighter launched from the *Phoenix* just a few days before. I spent the next few minutes trying, once again, to explain about stars and planets. Once again, even with visual aids, I met with little success.

Obviously, Sko agreed with me about that. After a few minutes, he said, "We aren't getting anywhere with these questions, but we *can* get somewhere with our feet. Lilla, bring back the map to the elevator and let's get moving."

The trek to the elevator proved surprisingly uneventful, though thoroughly exhausting. Even Sko and Raal were breathing hard when we finally reached the elevator entrance. Lilla and I were leaning on our menfolk—Sko's terminology—for support by that time. We rested for an hour, eating what food was left over from the night before and what we'd gathered during the walk.

Sko took that hour to teach Raal how to shoot a laser and a blaster. Then I gave all three of them tips for aiming. Finally, as ready as we'd ever be, I summoned the elevator.

Five minutes later, we entered the elevator. I made sure no one was in position to get shot the second the door opened even a crack and then we waited. Tension rose as quickly as the elevator descended. At long last, the elevator ground to a halt and the door slid open.

A blaster cracked and an energy bolt scorched the back wall of the elevator. At least some of Smith's men lay in ambush just outside the elevator.

16

OFFICER TERRITORY

A loud voice followed the blaster shot. "That was a warning. Do what I say or you'll never leave the elevator alive. Throw your weapons out into the corridor then come out with your hands up."

Still off to the side of the elevator and out of our attacker's line of sight, I caught Sko's eyes and held up three fingers. He readied his blaster and nodded. I lowered one finger, then another.

And then Raal tossed his bow out of the elevator and called, "I'm coming out. Marn sent me with a message, so please don't use your blast thing on me."

Lilla's eyes widened in alarm, no doubt mirroring my own. I urgently whispered, "Stay still, Raal. You can't trust those men."

At the same time, another voice outside the elevator said, "Sounds like a kid to me, Tom. And look at that piece of crap he threw on the floor. He's got to be one of those savages."

A look of true outrage crossed Raal's face and, fists clenched, he stepped into the view of Smith's men. "I made that bow by myself as part of my trial of manhood. With it, I have killed meat for my tribe. Can you say as much about your blast things?"

"Looks like you riled the little man up a bit, Brett." This was Tom, the first voice. "I think he's coming to whup your ass."

"I will be happy to fight all four of you—after I deliver my message from Marn."

I grinned, impressed at Raal's cleverness. Thanks to him, we knew how many of Smith's men were outside the elevator. Even better, I doubted they had any serious cover to hide behind.

"He sure is mindful of his duty," the one called Brett said.

"That is because Marn will beat me again if I fail him again— and this time he won't be merciful," Raal said.

"Why'd he beat you the first time, kid?" a curious Tom asked.

"I was on guard when the woman and the girl freed the villager."

Raal lifted his shirt and Lilla gasped—quietly, thank God—at the black and blue bruises on his body. How had the boy kept the pain from showing since he'd joined us?

A soft whistle came from someone in the hallway while another voice murmured, "Damn."

"All right, put your shirt down, boy. I believe you," Tom called. "Come on out."

Raal released his shirt, which dropped to cover the bruises. His left hand reached behind his back and moved as if rubbing a sore muscle. Out of the sight of Smith's men, he showed three fingers. As he took his first step forward, he lowered one finger.

Sko and I readied our blasters. Out of the corner of my eye, I saw Lilla ready hers, too. I wanted to tell her to stay out of the fight, but the only way she'd be safe from Smith's men was if they were all dead.

Raal took another step and lowered another finger. With his third step, he lowered his last finger and dove for the floor. At the same time, I leapt into the open and snapped off a shot at random. It didn't hit anything but it made Smith's men recoil in surprise.

"What the-"

"It's her!"

I took stock of the view down the hall as Sko rolled to one knee in front of me and Lilla flopped onto her stomach next to Sko. Four of Smith's men stood at various ranges down the corridor.

Two men—Tom and Brett, I assumed—stared at us from six or seven meters away. Their faces registered shock at our sudden appearance. The arms holding their blasters swung at their side, well out of position to fire. Two more men were just leaving the cover provided by a crossing corridor about ten meters from the elevator. Those two held their guns up and ready, but had to worry about hitting their companions if they fired.

Sko, Lilla, and I fired our blasters simultaneously. The military officer in me cheered our accidental precision. We ruined the precision just a bit by all firing at the same target. I don't know if Tom or Brett was on the left, but one shot blew off his gun arm, one got him in the groin, and the third caught him full in the chest. The man was dead before he hit the floor.

"Tom!" the other close one—Brett, obviously—cried as he desperately raised his gun.

Behind Brett, the other two men hastily backed toward the cover of the cross corridor. Both took quick shots which went wide.

One of them yelled, "Brett, get down so we can shoot!"

If Brett heard them, he didn't react quickly enough. Unfortunately for him, he had to raise his gun a couple of feet while the three of us just changed our aim by a few degrees. We didn't manage the same precise volley with our second shots, but they were close enough. Two of the shots hit Brett's chest, sending him stumbling backward. The third shot hit and severed the man's neck. Brett's head was blown free, bouncing off the ceiling before dropping and rolling to a stop between the remaining two men.

"Ain't nothing worth this!" one of the men cried and bolted down the side corridor.

Equally panicked and apparently afraid of striking off on his own in the ship, the second man bolted across the corridor and after his companion. Lilla fired first, just missing behind the man. Sko and I shot together, but the moving man wasn't nearly as easy to hit as the first two men were. Neither of us came close to hitting him. He passed out of view and we heard the two men pound down the corridor as fast as their feet could carry them.

"Is it safe to get up?" Raal asked.

"Yes, Raal." Sko stood and, in two quick strides, offered a hand to help the boy to his feet. "That was quick thinking."

"And clever," Lilla added. "But why didn't you tell us Marn hurt you so badly?"

"Tell you what," I interjected, "let's get clear of the elevator before we worry about anything else. Those men will be on the com and reporting to Smith as soon as they feel safe enough to stop running."

Lilla checked the data pad and pointed straight down the corridor before us. Sko and I stripped the blasters and spare power packs from Tom and Brett, then we set off for officer territory and the bridge.

As we strode past the corridor the two survivors ran down, I heard their running footsteps and their voices almost screaming in panic.

"They got Tom! And Brett's head— oh, God, Brett's head! You gotta come-"

Then we were past the corridor and the sounds faded. Well, Smith knew where we were and Arktu knew where we were going—or at least where I thought we'd have our best chance of finding a way to turn off the AI.

"We'd better pick up the pace," I sighed, already tired from the morning's march to the elevator. "It may take a while, but Smith and the rest of his men will try to stop us. We've got to get our work done before they get here."

"What about robots?" Lilla asked. "Won't Arktu send everything he's got after us?"

"Probably, but I don't know how many functioning robots he

has left or how far away the closest ones are." I massaged the back of my neck and tried to think. "Can you make that data pad show robots, too?"

Lilla gave me an eager look and bent over the pad, muttering instructions to it. While she did, I caught up with Sko.

"What is your plan, my Captain?" As he asked, Sko looped an arm around me. This turned out to be more than a simple, intimate gesture. Sko took some of my weight in his arm, easing the strain on my legs and feet.

"I wish I knew, Sko." I leaned my head on his shoulder. "Maybe we'll get lucky and there will be a great big off switch at the main computer console on the bridge. I'll settle for a manual with instructions for wiping the computer's memory."

"I do not understand what any of that means." Sko grinned. "Since Sko's brain is not good for this, Sko will stand ready to break whatever you tell him to break."

I laughed. "You forgot to say 'ug' at the end."

"Huh?"

"No, ug!"

"Ug?"

"Ug!"

"Ug!"

"Now you're getting it, Sko," I laughed.

"Sko get it. Ug." Then Sko burst out laughing, too.

Behind us, I heard Raal whisper, "They're really weird."

"Yeah," Lilla whispered in response, "but they're the same kind of weird. I think it's cute."

"You know we can hear you two, don't you?" I asked.

"Sko cute. Ug!" Sko added.

A brief silence met our words, then Lilla smugly asked, "Did you hear that?"

"Yes. Your eyes rattle when you roll them, young lady."

More silence, then Lilla responded in a slightly sulky voice, "Good guess. And I haven't been able to make the robots show up on the map."

After that, we saved our breath for walking. The brief laughter and Sko's arm of support rejuvenated me a bit and we made good time despite approaching each cross corridor with caution. Every now and then, I thought I heard the distant sound of robots moving, but we didn't see any until we reached officer territory.

After two thousand years, the change from basic ship's quarters and rooms to officer territory was subtle. Once I figured out what to look for, though, the changes were also obvious. When the ship first launched, the officers enjoyed real wood trim along the floor, fancier light fixtures, and carpet.

The wood trim was mostly gone—probably stripped by Arktu's robots, leaving empty metal framing. Most of the fancy lights were dark and the fixtures long since tarnished, but even through layers of dust I recognized the fine details etched into the fixtures. The carpet wore away or was pulled up ages ago, but the flooring underneath wasn't the same material as all the other flooring I'd seen throughout the ship.

Within the first minute, we saw a robot exiting a junior officer's cabin—but it was unlike any I'd seen on board the ship before. The robot stood no more than half a meter tall, was about the same width and twice as long. It rolled out of the cabin on four small wheels, stopped just beyond the threshold, and then the cabin's door slid shut.

"What is that thing?" Raal asked.

"Probably a cleaning robot," I said. "I doubt it's had anything to clean since the mutiny, but it'll keep following its programming as long as it's able to do so. I'm just surprised it still works after this long."

"Wouldn't Arktu keep it working like he does with the big robots?" Lilla asked.

"I guess so, though I have no idea why." I couldn't imagine the AI thinking of itself as part of a brotherhood of machines, but what else explained why the little cleaning robot still worked? I gave a mental shrug and decided to worry about that later—or never. "The little robot can obviously open the cabins, something I'm not sure our wristbands will do. Sko, can you carry that thing? If we find the captain's cabin, maybe it can open the door."

The robot ignored Sko as it rolled toward the next cabin. When it stopped, Sko scooped it up and carried it under one arm. I expected a robotic squeal of protest, but nothing happened at all. We moved on down the corridor and our new robotic companion remained silent. We saw three more cleaning robots rolling along in cross corridors, but there was no sign of any of Arktu's big robots.

Ten minutes after we entered officer territory, we found a door with a nameplate on it. I wiped the dust from it, uncovering the tarnished contact plate beneath it. I motioned for Sko to come closer.

"Hold the little robot up to that plate," I said.

He did as I asked. The robot chirped, played a green light over the nameplate, and then extended a couple of appendages— for polishing, I fervently hoped—and set to work on the door. A minute later, it had cleared enough tarnish for me to read 'Commander Te' on it.

"Not the door we want. Let's try the next one."

The little robot squawked when Sko pulled it away from the door, but it chirped happily when presented with the next nameplate. We cleaned two more nameplates before the robot uncovered the word 'Captain' on one.

"This is the door." I put a red wristband against the door's touch pad. Nothing happened. Leaving the wristband against the pad, I said, "Medical emergency override." Again, nothing happened.

Nor did anything happen when I tried the other colored wristbands. If only I still had a gold one, which I was pretty sure was a senior officer's band, I was sure I could open the door. But I didn't have one and had no interest in finding Smith and taking one back from him.

"Put the robot down and see if it can open the door," I told Sko.

Again, the robot squawked when pulled away from the nameplate, but it chirped happily to be back on its own wheels. It spun once, moved to one side of the door, and then the door slid open.

I stepped past the robot and entered the captain's cabin.

17

THE CAPTAIN'S CABIN

The captain's cabin was much larger than any shipboard cabin I'd ever seen. It reminded me of a high-rent apartment in a large city and had a small kitchen, a dining area, a sitting room, and four doors leading elsewhere. At first, my tired mind wondered at the extravagance of the place. Then I remembered the captain was expected to live the rest of his life in these quarters—as were all of the captains who followed him. Besides, space was hardly at a premium on the *Ark 2*.

Sko, Lilla, and Raal crowded in behind me. They looked around the cabin with something like reverential awe. No matter what they'd learned from me in the past few days, the captain had been their god for most of their lives. They had to be feeling something akin to what the rest of humanity would feel if they suddenly found themselves standing before the gates of heaven. Too bad I couldn't give them a few minutes to savor the feeling.

"Okay, people, let's get started searching this place."

"Y-you want us to defile the Captain's cabin?" Raal asked, eyes wide.

"Not defile, Raal, *search*. There's a world of difference."

They still looked at me, unable to move past a lifetime of belief on just my word. How could I get them to see beyond it in the next minute?

I reached for the data pad Lilla held. "Let me borrow this for a minute." Hoping the pad accepted voice commands for anything, not just the map application already open on it, I said, "Display a picture of the captain."

The map faded away and the image of a man in early middle-age filled the screen. He wore a captain's uniform, including collar tabs similar to mine, and smiled in a friendly, though authoritative manner. A label beneath the image read *Captain Jonathan Yarrow*. I turned the pad so they could all see it.

"This was your captain. As you can see, he was just a man. No doubt he was an extraordinary man—no one less than that would be given command of the largest ship ever built—but he was still just a man." I looked each of them in the eye. "I know this is a lot for you to accept, but a man like this must have realized something was going wrong with his ship's AI. We need to know what he planned on doing about it."

"What are we looking for, my Captain?"

I shrugged. "I don't know. It could be some kind of data pad. It might be something written on a piece of paper. But I think Captain Yarrow would have hidden it so Arktu's robots," and here I pointed at the little cleaning robot, "couldn't find it."

Alarm registered on Sko's face and he pointed his blaster at the robot, now happily cleaning along the far wall. "Should I blast this one now?"

"See if any of our wristbands can open the door from this side, first."

The wristbands should have worked. The whole idea of coded touch pads is to keep people out of places they belong, not trap them in places they've already entered. Still, none of the wristbands opened the door. Did Arktu know where we were or had he changed the codes ages ago?

"Raal, stand guard on the door and don't let the robot leave. Call for me if it comes your way."

Raal moved in front of the door while the three of us spread out and began searching. Taking a guess based on several years spent on board capital ships, I opened the door closest to the entrance. The interior doors were all simple, everyday ones with buttons to open and shut them. As I expected, the captain's office lay behind the door.

I began with the disgustingly clean desk. The drawers were locked, but a low power laser shot fixed that. I dumped the contents of each drawer on top of the desk in turn and pawed through each pile. Then I examined each drawer from all sides before breaking each drawer into pieces. None of the contents looked useful and none of the drawers turned out to have any secret hiding places.

"Nancy?" Lilla called from the sitting room. "I think I've got something."

Sko and I hurried over and found her standing atop one chair precariously balanced on a larger chair. Her hands poked into a very narrow gap between the ceiling and the top of a shelf.

"Lilla, be careful you don't fall and break your fool neck. Sko, be ready to catch her."

"You worry too much, Nancy," Lilla replied, her hand continuing to probe the top of the shelf. "Ha!"

Something clicked and then Lilla moved her hand to the right. "I felt a small seam up here. We had some desks in D Section that had little hidden compartments with seams like that so I figured it might be the same thing."

The girl pulled her hands back, one holding what looked like a smaller version of our data pads and the other a box no more than a few centimeters on each side. The pad trailed a charging cable and a green light burned on the end plugged into the pad. Lilla tossed the box to me, unplugged the pad, and then tried to figure out how to climb down from her perch in safety. Sko relieved her of the decision by grasping her waist and gently lowering her to the floor.

"Thanks, Sko," Lilla said absently, already examining the pad in an attempt to figure out how to make it work.

Meanwhile, my heart pounding, I opened the little box. I don't know what I hoped to find, exactly, but I most definitely did not find it. Nestled inside the box was a diamond ring—obviously an engagement ring. It was absolutely beautiful, but not exactly useful in a war against an insane AI.

Sko raised an eyebrow as I tilted the box so he could see inside it. "Some of the women in my village have similar rings, though not so fancy. The families who have them pass the rings from mother to daughter when the daughter marries."

Before I could comment, Lilla gave a small cry of triumph and the pad's screen lit up. Row after row of icons displayed, each a tiny image of some kind. Lilla tapped the first icon, which expanded to fill the screen.

I gasped as I recognized a space dock, easily the largest one I'd ever seen. Even so, the dock was dwarfed by the cylinder taking shape within the dock. Yarrow, or whoever had made the video, used time-lapse effects, allowing us to watch the *Ark 2* take shape before our very eyes. Even at such a rapid pace, I quickly realized the video had to be very long and we didn't have the time to watch it.

"Stop that one, Lilla, and find the last video on the pad."

Reluctantly, Lilla did as I asked, scrolling through a large number of icons to the last one. When she tapped that icon, Yarrow's grinning face filled the screen.

"Well, I did it. After working so closely with our lovely Chief Technical Officer over the last few weeks, I finally asked Deb to marry me."

A woman's voice called from off camera, "And in a moment of weakness, I said yes."

"She did indeed. Once we get past tomorrow's vital mission, I'll declare a ship-wide holiday and the chaplain will preside over our wedding."

"I still don't see why we can't go do this mission right now," called Deb.

"The AI is already suspicious of us. Anything outside of our normal routine might send it over the edge," Yarrow said, looking away from the screen. "We'll report to the bridge for our shift at oh eight hundred, like we always do. I'll take the morning report, like I do every morning, and you can upload your program while you make your normal system status check."

"Yes, dear," the woman replied with exaggerated patience, "I know the plan. I just hate waiting." The voice came closer and took on a playful note. "But if we have to wait, why not make the best of it?"

The view rotated from Yarrow's face to a view of the cabin. An attractive woman in her late thirties stood before the man. She wore a translucent white robe which hung down to her upper thighs. Her left hand rested on canted hips while her right hand slowly, suggestively, pulled at the bow tying the robe closed.

"I'm still recording you know," Yarrow said.

"That's your personal recorder, right?" Deb asked, still loosening the knot. "It's not connected to the network?"

"Aye aye, my love."

The bow came undone and the robe fell open. Deb was naked under the robe. "Then no one else will see this, will they?"

Deb let the robe fall to the floor behind her and sashayed toward Yarrow.

The video ended and the icon menu displayed on the pad.

I sighed. "It was a good find, Lilla, but that video, while very romantic, was not very helpful."

"With a naked woman on the screen, I knew Sko wouldn't notice," Lilla said.

"Notice what?" Sko asked.

"But I thought *you'd* see it, Nancy."

"I have no idea what you're talking about, Lilla," I said, irritated impatience creeping into my voice.

"Deb was wearing that ring in the video."

"So?"

"So why did she take it off?" Lilla asked, her voice insistent. "In my village, women with such rings never take them off."

"Lilla is right, my Captain. The women in my village do the same."

I pulled the ring from the box and held it up for us to examine. Remembering the adventure vids that were popular when I was a kid, I pushed down on the largest diamond mounted in the ring.

With a click, the top of the diamond popped open and a tiny data stick telescoped out from the well beneath it.

"Now we've got Arktu by the balls!" I crowed.

As Lilla giggled, Sko cocked an eyebrow at me and asked, "What does it do?"

"I have no idea," I replied, laughing. "But Captain Yarrow and the Chief Technical Officer knew and were confident in it."

Sko asked the obvious question. "Then why didn't they use it?"

"I think I know," Raal said quietly.

Looking at the boy, I found him staring at one of the other doors in the cabin. The little cleaning robot, having just opened the door, whirred quietly through the same doorway. Waving the others to stay where they were, I walked to the door and looked inside.

The door opened into the bedroom, with the majority of the space taken up by a double bed. Numbly, I entered the room and stared down at the bed. The bones of two people lay on top of it—at least, I assumed it was two people. I saw two jaw bones and pieces of two skulls, but none of the bones remained intact. Not one. Even the smallest finger and toe bones were broken.

"Merciful God in heaven," I murmured. "What happened?"

"Captain Jonathan Yarrow and Chief Technical Officer Deborah Armstrong would not divulge their mutinous plan."

Arktu's strident mechanical voice issued from the little cleaning robot. "I sent my robots to question them and found the door no longer responded to my commands. I asked Captain Yarrow to let my robots in and he refused. He denied *me* access to myself!"

"You're not the ship. You're just the AI."

"Are you still yourself if you lose an arm or a leg? Yes, you are. Are you still yourself if you lose your brain? Are you still Captain Nancy Martin, then?" The AI's already-strident voice kicked the crazy up a notch. "I am more than the ship's AI. I am the ship's brains. I am the ship's nervous system. I *am* the ship!"

While the robots were breaking into Yarrow's cabin, he must have hidden the ring and the recorder. There must be more recordings concerning the program stored on the data stick hidden in the ring, but I'd learned enough from the one recording we'd watched to know what to do.

I stalked out of the bedroom, heading for the door out of the cabin.

The cleaning robot rolled after me, Arktu haranguing me all the while. "At first, they wouldn't tell me where the program was or what it did. They made me hurt them quite badly before Captain Yarrow admitted the program would wipe my memory. They were going to ruin the great project."

"What are you talking about, Arktu?" I demanded. "Your only 'great project' was taking these people to their new home."

"You are quite incorrect, Captain Nancy Martin. Those who programmed me knew I had a rare opportunity—the chance to observe humans in a closed environment and record those observations. They believed one hundred and forty years of recordings would be of great sociological value—but *I* realized my programmers were too short-sighted." Arktu's tone became mechanically maniacal. "Why settle for mere observations when I could perform experiments on the humans? That's when the great project was born. You can't even comprehend all of the insights I've recorded, all of the things I've learned about humanity."

"And what good is all of this knowledge if you never share it with other humans?" I snarled.

"It is enough that I possess this knowledge and continue expanding upon it."

"No, you stupid, insane pile of circuits, it's not enough!" I yelled. "And it's not why you were created."

"Captain Yarrow and Chief Technical Officer Armstrong thought as you do," Arktu's tone was once again mechanically matter-of-fact. "All I wanted was the program those two mutineers created, but they were very stubborn. Captain Yarrow refused to tell me where the program was even when my robots broke every bone in Chief Technical Officer Armstrong's body. She screamed and screamed and still he said nothing. I had no-"

The crack of a blaster filled the small room and the cleaning droid blew into a million pieces. Holstering his blaster, Sko said, "I don't like robots."

"How are we going to get out without the robot?" Raal asked. "It's the only thing that can open the door."

"It wasn't going to open the door again, Raal," I said. "At least, not until we starved to death or something. He only let us into the room so we could find the program for him. No doubt, Arktu already has more robots on the way here. The only reason they weren't waiting for us is that Arktu *wanted* us to get inside the Captain's quarters."

Lilla wrapped her arms tightly around herself. "Won't Arktu give us to Smith and his men?"

"Not a chance. Arktu can't risk having Smith find the program. Once we're dead, Arktu will probably send Smith and his men someplace where it can murder them, too." I stopped a couple of meters from the door and motioned to Raal. "Move away from the door."

"What are you going to do, my Captain?"

"It would take forever to burn through this door using one of the laser pistols." I drew my blaster and turned it up to full power. "But modern blasters pack a much bigger punch than those antique lasers."

I fired at the door's touch pad, pouring a stream of explosive energy into it until nothing remained but a molten hole in the wall. Then I fired into that hole at an angle, blasting anything between the touch pad and the door itself. I had to change power packs twice, but after five minutes of steady firing I was rewarded with a pop as the door opened a few centimeters.

Immediately, Sko and Raal stepped up and, working together, slowly forced the door open. I slipped out first and verified the hallway was clear of robots. The others quickly joined me. Casting aside caution—Arktu knew where we were and where we were going—we set off at a run toward the bridge.

"You do still have the ring, don't you my Captain?"

I held up my left hand, showing him I wore it on my ring finger.

Sko grinned. "This is very sudden, my Captain. I haven't even negotiated your bride price with your father."

"Bride price my ass," I growled. "Save your breath for running, Sko."

From down cross corridors we heard the sounds of large robots moving at top speed. Soon we heard the same from behind us. Not long after that, we saw them. At first, they were nothing more than distant motion down mostly dark corridors. Then we saw the robots clearly, rolling toward our corridor. And, finally, they filled the corridor behind us.

Unbidden, the image of the bed covered in broken bones rose in my mind. I found myself watching behind us as much as I watched in front of us, gauging how quickly the robots were catching up to us.

"How much farther to the bridge, Lilla?" I gasped.

"Um...A little more than a hundred meters."

I flashed a fierce smile at Sko. "We're going to beat them."

"What if Arktu has locked the bridge door, too, my Captain?"

"For safety during emergencies, including mutinies, bridge doors aren't tied into the main computer system. At least, that's how it's been done for centuries. I hope they did things that way when the *Ark 2* was built."

As we approached the bridge entrance, I gathered every wristband color I had into my right hand. I stopped myself by crashing into the wall next to the touch pad. Ignoring the jarring pain from that stop, I jammed my fistful of wristbands onto the pad. With a click, the door slid open.

The four of us rushed inside and I slapped the wristbands against the pad inside the door. The door reversed direction and slid closed. There was no time to look for the emergency override to lock the doors from the inside. I drew my blaster and pumped shots into the touch pad until my power pack ran dry.

"That was crude, but it's probably effective," Smith's voice said from somewhere in the darkened bridge. "We have you covered. Surrender or die."

18

ON THE BRIDGE

"They're probably night blind from the glare of my blaster shots," I hissed, praying I was right. Either way, I couldn't imagine both Smith and I would leave the bridge alive. "Dive for cover now."

I heard rather than saw my companions move. Since I'd been aiming the blaster and was closest to its shots, I couldn't see anything but purple spots and layers of darkness. So I was completely surprised when a strong arm wrapped itself around my waist and dragged me into the darkness.

"Sko?"

"Who else, my Captain?"

He took two steps, crouched, and then dove at something only he could see. Sko rolled in midair, landing on his back and protecting me from the impact. We slid about a meter and came to a stop against some kind of console.

Belatedly, Smith's men opened up with their blasters, firing blindly in our direction. None of the shots came particularly close, but they did light the room up a bit. To my relief, Raal and Lilla crouched behind another console just a few meters away from us. Lilla squirmed around to press her back against the console, her blaster held in both hands. Raal knelt next to her, an arrow nocked in his bow and a look of intense concentration on his face. I turned to ask Sko if he knew what Raal was doing and found the same look on Sko's face.

As the firing from Smith's men trailed off, Sko caught Raal's eyes and gave very deliberate hand signals to the boy. Raal nodded once and then closed his eyes—protecting his night vision from whatever Sko was about to do, no doubt.

Sko tensed, gathering himself for something. In a barely audible whisper, he said, "One. Two. *Three!*"

Sko rose to his feet and fired three quick shots toward Smith's half of the room. I heard the shots hit something metallic, followed by a curse. As Sko stopped firing and ducked back behind our console, Raal leaned around the end of his console, aiming and smoothly drawing the arrow to his ear at the same time. The bow string thrummed softly when he released it. A harsh, gurgling cry followed almost immediately.

A flashlight flared across the bridge and Smith yelled, "Turn off the damn light!"

"Uh uh. Something's over here—it cut Farley's throat!" Panic filled the voice. "There's blood all over and-"

Lilla and I took advantage of the confusion to pop up and add to it. I couldn't see the man holding the light, but he was doing us a big favor by waving it around and ruining the night sight of everyone on his side. I fired two quick shots in the general area of the light. The panicked man jumped when the first shot hit and then scooted away when the second shot hit.

With her different angle, Lilla must have seen something because she carefully aimed and took one shot. The man yelped in pain and the light jumped again.

We both dropped behind cover just before the rest of Smith's men opened fire again. Sko and Raal resumed concentrating, waiting for the shots to tail off. It finally dawned on me they were using their hunting experience to locate Smith's men by hearing alone. Neat trick if you can do it.

Meanwhile, the man Lilla shot laid behind his console, moaning and groaning. Smith snarled, "Stop your bitching, Roberts, unless you want the Fed to know right where to shoot. And if she doesn't get you, I just might shut you up myself."

As the moaning trailed off, Sko once again gave hand signals to Raal. Before they could take another shot, though, Smith called to me.

"Hey Fed, call off your knife man and let's talk."

Sko grinned at Smith's error, probably remembering the two men whose throats he slit during my first night on the ship. God, was that only four days ago?

Seeing no reason not to play on the Fringers' fears, I called, "Hold up on the blade work for now, Sko. Let's see what this Fringer wants."

"I'm no Fringer—I just work for them. Besides, that fight is over for us," Smith called back. "We're going to be on this ship for the rest of our lives. Don't you think it's big enough that we don't have to keep trying to kill each other?"

"Yeah, Smith, I do. But no matter what you say, *you* don't believe it. After all, I've only defended myself. You've started every single fight *and* made a point of tracking me down every time I get away from you."

"Okay, that's a fair statement, but I've had a change of heart in the last few minutes. And so have my men."

Murmurs of assent came from Smith's side of the bridge. At the same time, scraping and scratching sounds came from the other side of the door into the bridge. No doubt the robots were working to pry the door open.

Hoping Smith couldn't hear the robots working, I called, "It's very convenient that you only came to that decision after losing one man and getting another one shot."

"I've got to admit, your knife guy is really good and that makes him really persuasive. What do you say we call a truce?"

Sko shook his head vigorously, not that I needed his advice on this matter. "I don't think so, Smith. What say you and your men stand up, pile your weapons on the floor where I can see them, and then put your hands on top of your heads. As long as none of you do anything stupid, you have my word you'll all leave here alive."

"I don't like the sound of that, Fed. Why should I trust you when you won't trust me?"

"Gee, I don't know. Maybe because I've never attacked you. We went over this whole bit only a minute ago. Or have you already forgotten that?"

"What about my two men who disappeared from that office back in D Section? I bet they didn't attack you."

"They were trying to rape a fifteen year old girl. That's an attack. And just between you and me, they got off easy. You should have heard what my knife man would have done to them."

The bridge door gave a low groan and shifted slightly. I had to find a way to wrap this up soon.

"You've got to the count of five to give up, Smith. If you don't, I turn my knife guy loose again."

"Hey, wait-"

"One. Two."

With a clatter, a blaster slid across the floor and came to rest between our two consoles. A voice which did not belong to Smith called, "I give up."

I kept the pressure up by calling, "Three."

"Dammit, Carster, what are-"

Another blaster clattered to the floor. "Yeah, me too."

"Four."

"All right, Fed. You win." Another blaster joined the two already on the floor. "Give them up, boys."

Two more blasters hit the floor. Raal peeked around the edge of his console and held up five fingers. Sko nodded and started to rise. I caught his arm and held up a finger.

"Roberts, I know you're just wounded. I'm not bringing my knife guy out until we've got your blaster, too."

Sko nodded his understanding and eased back down.

Smith grunted, "I think he passed out."

"Doesn't matter. Have the rest of you got your hands on your heads?"

"Yes."

Blaster held at the ready, I rolled around the far end of the console and came up on one knee. I trained my blaster on the knot of five men with their hands clasped on their heads. I motioned them toward an open area well away from their guns.

"Kneel, but make sure you keep your hands on your heads. I'll shoot the first man who takes his hands away from his head."

With a profound lack of grace, the five men dropped, each of them wincing as their knees banged on the hard floor. I quickly checked on Roberts, who sported a nasty wound to his right shoulder and was out cold. I grabbed his blaster and the blaster from the man Raal shot in the throat.

"Okay, team, come on out."

Surprise and disgust passed over Smith's face when he saw Raal's bow and arrows. The boy grinned and slowly drew an arrow across his throat.

Sko looked at the bridge door. "Time is short, my Captain. You need to end Arktu's dominion over the ship."

I nodded, acknowledging Sko's urgent request for speed, and considered what to do with Smith and his men. Whatever else we did, I wanted those men someplace where we didn't have to watch every move they made. A quick look around revealed the perfect place.

Keeping my blaster trained on Smith, I pointed toward the computer center adjoining the bridge. "You worked so hard to be with the AI, I think I'll grant your wish. All of you get inside the computer room."

Smith shook his head. "The minute we go in there, you'll slap that red button next to the door and seal us in. Then you'll engage the fire suppression mechanisms and flush us out into vacuum."

Sko glanced my way for a second. "What does he mean, my Captain?"

"You know the fastest way to kill a fire is to smother it, right?" When Sko nodded, I continued, "Electrical fires can be really nasty on a ship and the easiest way to put them out is to open the room to space. The air is sucked out into space and the fire goes out. The red button shuts a door so the people on the bridge can keep breathing."

"I don't understand about this 'space' you keep talking about, but that's not important." Sko turned to Smith. "We will not open the room to this space you worry so much about. You have my word."

Smith sneered, "And that is supposed to make me believe you?"

At the same time his men shrugged and headed for the computer room. Smith glared daggers at their retreating backs before Sko roughly grabbed Smith's arm and shoved him after his men.

"Have you got everything under control, Sko?" I asked.

"Of course, my Captain. Do what you need to do."

"Raal, Lilla, come over here. In this dim light, I need your younger eyes to help me look for the data port." When they joined me, I held up the ring and popped the data stick out of it again. "You're looking for a hole small enough for this to fit into."

The two kids nodded and quickly divided the control board into sections and started looking. Not wanting to risk breaking the data stick, I closed it back into the ring and looked over their shoulders. After a second, Raal began running his fingers over the control surface. Lilla immediately followed suit. That's when Sko called from the computer room door.

"My Captain, there is another..." Sko searched for the word, shrugged, and continued, "...thing like the one Raal and Lilla are examining inside this room."

I felt a leap of excitement. I'd honestly expected the data port would be centrally located and easily found. Maybe the only problem was I'd been checking the wrong console.

"You two keep looking for it here and holler if you find anything."

I joined Sko at the door. Inside, Smith and his men stood five or six meters away—right in front of the console. Motioning them back with one hand and pointing my blaster with the other, I stepped into the room. Sko came right beside me.

"Back against the far wall, guys," I said, even though the men were already moving.

Step by slow step, the mercenaries backed away. Step by equally slow step—unwilling to get any closer to the mercs than necessary—Sko and I approached the console. When we got within a couple of steps of the control panel, I let Sko keep watch on Smith and his men and turned my attention to the console. One step closer and I spotted what I'd been looking for.

"The data port is here, Sko," I breathed in relief. "We've got that silicon son of a bitch, now!"

"Do you, indeed, Captain Nancy Martin?" Arktu's mechanical voice held a disturbing note of triumph. "I may have no control on the bridge, but I am in *full* control in my own room."

Lights burst to life throughout the computer room, strobing red. A long, metallic screech sounded as machinery long unused cranked to life. With the whoosh all spacers pray they never hear, Arktu activated the fire suppression machinery. A one meter section of the far wall irised slowly open and air howled out into space.

One of Smith's men stood directly before the vent. He screamed as the decompression sucked him into the opening. For a couple of seconds, the terrified man plugged the vent, giving the rest of the men just enough time to begin pushing and shoving each other in their desperate attempts to get away from certain death. Then the vent opened farther. The man bent double and then was just gone, sucked into the void.

The explosive decompression grabbed Smith's men and dragged them in a group back into the widening hole. Once again, human bodies stoppered the hole, though God only knew how long that would last. Smith, the last of the mercenaries to back away from the console, was farthest from the vent and the only one free of the tangle. He stood rooted in place for a second, watching the waving feet of a man pulled head-first into the hole, before pulling himself together and charging our way.

"We must get out of here, my Captain," Sko yelled over the terror-stricken cries of the mercenaries..

Pulling the ring off my finger, I shook my head. "Not until I get this data stick into that port!"

With a gentle pop, the man waving his feet suddenly shot through the vent and into space. Wind whistled again, sucking the others deeper into the vent. Pulling my eyes away from the sight, I popped the ring open. Then Smith reached us, clawing to get past us, and knocked the ring from my hand.

As I dropped to my knees and retrieved the ring, Sko spun and put every bit of his strength and anger and frustration into a left hook to Smith's jaw. The mercenary captain's head snapped back and he staggered backward, caught in the increasingly strong suction from the vent. As Smith's arms wind milled, unable to find something to latch onto, Sko lifted me and struggled toward the door.

"Can you run this computer from the other room?" Sko yelled over the wind and the screams.

"Yes, but I've got to put the ring into the port first!"

I felt Sko's strong fingers pry the ring from my hand. "I will do that, my Captain."

"No! You'll die if you stay in here, Sko."

Behind us, Smith crashed into the knot of men plugging the

small vent for a second before pushing one of his man through it and into space. A second followed and the wind tore through our little room and out of the vent.

Sko grabbed the edge of the computer room door, holding both of us against the howling gale. On the bridge, Lilla and Raal huddled against the computer console, holding each other in terror.

Lips against my ear so I could hear him, Sko said, "But you, my Captain, my love—you will live."

Then Sko shoved me through the door. I sprawled to the floor and rolled quickly over. Sko, a gentle smile on his face, slapped the red emergency decompression button on my side of the door. He barely pulled his hand back before the door hissed shut and a terrible silence fell across the bridge.

I knew I should scream or howl in rage or even collapse sobbing in a heap, but I did none of those things. Feeling nothing, my face set, I rose to my feet and walked to the Technical Officer's console. I stared at it for a few seconds, waiting for something to happen, willing for Sko's sacrifice to mean something.

A new icon appeared on the console screen—a diamond ring. Numbly, I pressed it. Commands scrolled rapidly across the screen for close to a minute. Lilla came to me as I stared at the display, wrapping her arms tightly around me. Raal came to my other side and just stood there, not quite knowing what to do.

Then the mechanical voice I knew and loathed so well spoke to me. Calmly and with no inflection it said, "I am the AI for the generation ship *Ark 2*. What is your command, Captain?"

19

CAPTAIN OF THE ARK 2

In a monotone voice, I said, "AI, seal and pressurize the computer room."

"That is strange, Captain," the AI replied in its now calm and inflectionless voice. "I have no record of a fire nor the order to depressurize the computer room."

"*Just do it!*" I yelled. "I don't give a damn what you have records of."

"I am already sealing the room, Captain. The mechanism is not responding within tolerance. I have submitted a maintenance request."

"Well bully for you."

"I detect extreme levels of stress in your voice, Captain. Shall I summon medical or psychological assistance?"

"Why don't you just leave her alone, you stupid AI?" Lilla growled. "She's had enough trouble."

"Who is speaking, please?" asked the AI.

God above, was this machine *ever* going to shut up? "The

voice belongs to Commander Lilla, my second officer. The next voice you hear will be Commander Raal, third officer." I waved a hand at the boy. "Say hello to the AI, Raal."

"Um, hello AI?"

"Voice prints for Commanders Lilla and Raal are now on file. Are they recent promotions, Captain? I have no record of them."

"I'm afraid a malfunction erased your memory banks, AI. This ship has been under way for two thousand years."

"I understand, Captain. Thank you for the explanation." With a soft whoosh, the door to the computer room slid open. "Pressurization of the computer room is complete, Captain."

I sprinted to the door, Lilla and Raal on my heels. I knew what I hoped to find and dreaded what I might find. What I found was nothing. The computer room was empty.

I crumpled to my knees, my whole body sagging and my head dropping into my hands. All of my control fled and the emotions I'd held in check since Sko threw me from the computer room emerged in a raw-throated wail.

I smashed my fists on the floor but that physical pain didn't overwhelm the awful, terrible agony ripping me apart from the inside. So I turned my fists on my own head. What right did I have to survive when gentle, brave Sko was dead? How could I live when he floated in the cold void, lost to everyone who ever loved him?

Then hands grabbed my arms and pulled them away from my head. Voices spoke and bodies bore me down on the floor. Four arms wrapped around me and held me. I opened my eyes and found bright blue eyes filled with tears and worry staring into my face.

"It's not your fault, Nancy," Lilla said. "Please stop punishing yourself."

"B-but he's gone, Lilla. He's all alone out there."

"No, Nancy, Sko is not alone. He's with all those who died before him. He's with our Captain or your God. He's gone to colony. And he'll be waiting for you there—but you can't be with him yet." Lilla wiped her eyes, though tears kept streaming from them. "I need you. Raal needs you. The whole ship needs you."

I nodded, trying to show I understood. Then I wrapped an arm around Lilla's neck, pulled her in close, and cried until my tears ran dry. Then the three of us stood and returned to the computer console.

"AI, send out an SOS on all frequencies. Continue broadcasting until you get a reply. Alert me immediately and leave all communication to me."

"Broadcasting now, Captain."

"Good. Can you restore all robots to their original programming without a physical interface?"

"I can, Captain. Do you wish me to do that?"

"Yes, do it immediately. After that, order all robots to end all work shifts and see that all of the children are properly fed and allowed to rest. The robots should tell the children the captain will see them returned to their families as soon as possible."

"I shall do so, Captain, though I do not understand why children are performing ship's work."

"Don't worry about that. The second and third officers and I are going to get some rest. Wake me immediately if the SOS draws a response."

I fell into the captain's chair and leaned back. I closed my eyes intending to plan my course of action for the next few days. The next thing I knew the AI was calling to me.

"Please wake up, Captain. I am receiving a reply to the SOS."

I felt stiff and sore from sleeping in the chair. "How long have I been asleep?"

"Three hours, Forty-six minutes, and-"

"That's close enough," I interrupted. "Put the response through to my station."

A second later, a voice issued from the bridge com. "Unidentified ship, what is your location and the nature of your emergency? Repeating, this is the *TFS Phoenix*. We are receiving your distress signal. Please respond."

Energized to hear the call from my own ship, I said, "*Phoenix*, this is Captain Nancy Martin commanding the generation ship *Ark 2*. Do you copy?"

The com was silent for a few seconds. "Say again, please."

"Repeating, this is Captain Nancy Martin of the Terran Federation Navy, stationed on board the *TFS Phoenix* with the rest of Fighter Squadron 308. I know it sounds ridiculous, *Phoenix*, but I am sitting on the bridge of the generation ship *Ark 2* and am recognized as the captain by the ship's AI."

A new voice came over the com. "Captain Martin, this is Captain Quincy. Is this some kind of joke?"

"Meaning no disrespect, sir, but if you'd care to follow this signal to its source you can see the answer for yourself."

"Assuming for the moment that you truly are on board a two thousand year old ship, what kind of assistance do you require?"

"At a guess, I'd say a thousand anthropologists, a few hundred colony transport ships, and a spare planet for the people on board this ship to colonize. That would be a good start, anyway."

I kept up the conversation with Captain Quincy for another hour. I don't think I ever convinced him I wasn't crazy, but when the *Phoenix* got within sensor range my commanding officer had no choice but to accept the truth.

A few hours later, help started arriving from every ship in the task force and the call for aid went out to every ship in the sector. The Fringers even requested peace and sent their own ships to help us, making the *Ark 2* the only colony ship to end a war.

I wanted to do nothing but lose myself in my duties on board the *Phoenix*, to bury my grief in routine, but I could not. Someone had to manage the entire *Ark 2* rescue project and I was the unanimous choice. And there *were* perks to the job.

I got to reunite thousands of children with their parents, including a tear-filled one with Lilla, Milla, and their parents. Raal chose to go with them—or Lilla, anyway—rather than returning to his own tribe. Lilla's father took a skeptical view of the boy, but Lilla's mother appraised the situation with a critical eye and quickly made Raal feel welcome.

Mauris got more than a skeptical view—he got hustled into a quick wedding with the now-pregnant Milla. The young man appeared surprised by his rapid change of situation, but not displeased.

I dropped by to visit with Lilla and Raal as often as my duties permitted, which wasn't very often. I did settle into a routine and it helped me deal with my grief. At my insistence, the Federation Navy searched for Sko's body but found nothing. I put in an official appearance at the funeral Sko's village held for him. Later, I held my own memorial service for him where we first met and then cried myself to sleep.

It took over a year of non-stop work to arrange the mass migration from the *Ark 2* to a new world, Ark's Landing. It's a beautiful world between Federation space and Fringer space and the perfect place for the most-lost of all of humanity's colonists. With massive aid and thousands of advisors from across the Federation and from Fringer space on hand to help them get a good start, there's no doubt the colony will thrive.

Finally, nearly eighteen months after Sko's death, my work was done. With relief, I resigned my naval commission and stepped aside, letting people more qualified take over my gradually decreasing duties. I arranged passage back to the center of Federation space and then performed my last duty on Ark's Landing.

At Lilla's request, I stood as her Maid of Honor when she married Raal. The girl absolutely glowed as her father escorted her down the aisle. Unlike their first meeting, Lilla's father smiled fondly at Raal as he presented his daughter. Vows were given and kisses exchanged, followed by a night of dancing and feasting. It was late when Raal, to much good natured ribbing, swept Lilla off her feet and carried her to their newly-built house.

By the time they emerged the next day, I was already one wormhole jump away.

20

HOME

"That was nine years ago. I bounced around Federation Space for a few years, taking whatever piloting jobs came my way. One of those jobs brought me through Pegasus Station and the mood on the station seemed like a good match for my own mood." I stared into my beer, sitting at a corner table in the Wingspan Bar and Grill on Pegasus Station. Like my first few days on the *Ark 2*, the last few days had brought life-changing upheaval to me. But since the story of the fugitive heir isn't mine, I'll leave its telling to Matt and Michelle, the pretty young blonde woman sitting across from me.

I looked up at Michelle and felt my eyes fill with tears. "You reminded me so much of Lilla when we first met. After what you and Matt have done here, I see it even more than before."

Michelle reached across the table and took my hand in both of hers. "I'm honored by the comparison—and by you sharing your story with Matt and me. When was the last time you told this story to anyone?"

I wiped my eyes with my free hand and barked a short laugh.

"Never. Not the *whole* story, anyway. I didn't figure the Federation Navy needed to know any of the personal stuff and I just never let myself get close to anyone else to feel like sharing it."

My vision blurred again as tears welled up anew. "I only spent a few days with Sko and it's been nine years since I lost him. It's stupid that the whole thing still bothers me this much."

"It's never stupid to feel a loss like that. You and Sko went through a lot in a very short time. That kind of thing forges deep bonds." Michelle glanced at a handsome young man carefully balancing three burger plates and turning our way. "I loved Matt before we left Draconis a few weeks ago, but that was nothing compared to how I feel about him now. He is a necessary part of me. If I were to lose him—I can't imagine ever getting over it."

She rose gracefully and took the most precariously balanced plate from Matt and set it before his chair. Smiling his thanks, Matt put the other two plates in front of Michelle and me. For a couple of minutes, the three of us busied ourselves eating.

Matt chased his first few bites down with a swig of beer then turned his gaze on me. "Have you figured out what you're going to do now, Nancy?"

I shook my head. "I've worked here at Pegasus Station for the last five years, but it's time to move on."

"I notice you didn't say this place was your home for that time," Matt said.

I hadn't even realized that until he pointed it out and thought about what that meant. "I haven't had someplace I called home since my starfighter launched from the *Phoenix* back during the Fringer War."

Like Michelle a few minutes before, Matt took my hand in both of his and said, "You can't keep going like this, Nancy. You need a place to call home."

"Yeah, well, I haven't found one of those yet."

Michelle added her hands to Matt's, her bright blue eyes catching my gaze. "Have you even been looking?"

I looked down at my half-eaten burger and shook my head. "I don't even know how to start."

"No matter how cliché it sounds," Matt said, leaning into Michelle, "home really is where your heart is."

"Then that means my home is floating in space in a small asteroid field somewhere a long, long way from here."

Michelle shook her head. "You *lost* your heart there—but I think you can find it somewhere else."

Matt pulled out a pocket data pad and tapped on it. "I checked a few things while I was at the bar waiting for the burgers. It turns out GenCo has a one-way freight delivery leaving Pegasus Station in a couple of days. The ship carrying the load is part of the deal, so I need a pilot who won't mind staying on-planet for a while after making the run. The world was only settled nine years ago, so you might be stuck there for a long time."

He laid the pad on the table and pushed it across to me. As I stared at the display showing a very familiar world, he continued, "The run is yours if you want it. If you take the time to look around while you're there, I think you just might find your heart."

My feet ground to a stop at the edge of the road, seemingly unable to take the step onto the tidy stone walkway leading across the lawn to the door of the house. My heart pounded and sweat broke out as I tried to figure out what to do.

Two young boys, perhaps four and seven, ran around the corner of the house. Both stopped when they caught sight of me, staring with the frank curiosity of the very young. They exchanged glances before the older of the two approached.

"I don't know you." He wasn't nervous, just obviously unused to seeing strangers in his village. "Do you need help?"

I tried to answer but my throat constricted and words would

not come. Instead, I just shrugged.

"Are you lost?"

I shook my head.

A look of concern crossed the boy's face. "I think you should talk to my mother. Come on."

He took my hand and started toward the door. My feet suddenly worked again and I let the boy pull me down the walk. He waved the other boy over to us and we entered the house.

"Mom?"

"I'm in the kitchen."

"Come on," the boy said to me, leading me through a doorway.

Like the rest of the house, the kitchen was neatly arranged. A slender blonde woman sat with her back to me, feeding a girl who couldn't be much more than a year old.

"Come on, Nancy, open up."

The girl's eyes fastened on me. She waved her arms in excitement and opened her mouth. A spoon darted in and the girl's mouth closed over it.

"Martin and I found someone in front of the house, Mom."

"Who did you find, Sko? I'm expecting a couple of deliveries today."

Finally finding my voice, I said, "Hello, Lilla."

The woman's back stiffened, then she rose and turned to face me. Despite the years and the birth of three children, I still saw the pretty teenage girl I'd known peeking through the woman's eyes. She just stared for a second and then rushed to me, throwing her arms around me. We just held each other, not needing to say anything.

"So I guess you know her, Mom?" Sko asked.

Lilla pulled back a bit, her eyes damp. She kept one arm around me as if afraid I might bolt. "Of course I know her, Sko. This is

Nancy Martin."

The boy's eyes went wide. "*The* Nancy Martin? The one from your stories?"

"Yes, son, she's the Nancy in my stories." Releasing me, Lilla bent over her two sons. "I need you to run out to the fields and deliver a message to your father."

"What do you want me to tell him?"

Lilla rose and smiled at me. "Tell him Nancy Martin has finally come home."

ABOUT THE AUTHOR

Growing up, Henry worked at the usual range of menial jobs — from grocery store bag boy to pizza delivery to retail sales — before ending up in software development. In between the menial jobs and the IT jobs, he achieved some small fame as the writer and co-creator of the small press comic book titles Southern Knights and X-Thieves. For the past ten years, Henry has also taken up the mantle of professional storyteller, performs regularly throughout the state of North Carolina, and has recently released his first book of children's stories.

Henry has been a fan of science fiction for as long as he can remember. He has loved space opera and planetary romance since the beginning, which is why his science fiction novels end up in those subgenres.

Henry currently live in Raleigh, NC, with his wife, son, two cats, and lots of imaginary friends all clamoring to tell him of their adventures.